...t easy for Eric T... ...mettle.
There ...e four buses in the drivew... ...azzi in the trees, the money's running out (again) and the new album is seriously late. Eric's kids Buddy and Lou need to take control – otherwise it's like the End . . .

Ladies and gentlemen, if you were Buddy and Lou Thrashmettle, what would you do?
a) Knit brand-new underwear from the fur of fluffy kittens to make sure you don't get cold when you're evicted from the Thrashmettle mansion
b) Twiddle your thumbs
c) Get your dad to buy a haunted castle/recording studio, move in, get LOUD and get things sorted

Buddy and Lou are not twiddlers or knitters. They are good at taking action – even when there's at least one ghost and some very strange people from the Republic of Hongania trying to stop them. Read on!

Sam Llewellyn is the author of many quite brilliant books for adults and children, including three about the delightful Darling children, and The Return of Death Eric, *the first book about the world's favourite rock genius. It is sad but true that Sam himself was very nearly a rock star, and can still be spotted playing the guitar loudly in some very odd places.*

THE
HAUNTING
OF
DEATH ERIC

SAM LLEWELLYN

PUFFIN

445778

PUFFIN BOOKS

Published by the Penguin Group

Penguin Books Ltd, 80 Strand, London WC2R 0RL, England

Penguin Group (USA) Inc., 375 Hudson Street, New York, New York 10014, USA

Penguin Group (Canada), 90 Eglinton Avenue East, Suite 700, Toronto, Ontario, Canada M4P 2Y3
(a division of Pearson Penguin Canada Inc.)

Penguin Ireland, 25 St Stephen's Green, Dublin 2, Ireland (a division of Penguin Books Ltd)

Penguin Group (Australia), 250 Camberwell Road, Camberwell, Victoria 3124, Australia
(a division of Pearson Australia Group Pty Ltd)

Penguin Books India Pvt Ltd, 11 Community Centre, Panchsheel Park, New Delhi – 110 017, India

Penguin Group (NZ), 67 Apollo Drive, Mairangi Bay, Albany, Auckland 1310, New Zealand
(a division of Pearson New Zealand Ltd)

Penguin Books (South Africa) (Pty) Ltd, 24 Sturdee Avenue, Rosebank, Johannesburg 2196, South
Africa

Penguin Books Ltd, Registered Offices: 80 Strand, London WC2R 0RL, England

penguin.com

Published 2006

1

Set in Baskerville MT

Typeset by Palimpsest Book Production Limited, Grangemouth, Stirlingshire
Made and printed in England by Clays Ltd, St Ives plc

British Library Cataloguing in Publication Data
A CIP catalogue record for this book is available from the British Library

ISBN-13: 978-0-141-31984-1
ISBN-10: 0-141-31984-4

For Toby 'Smiley Eyes' Parker
and
The Canterville Ghost

INTRO

Night was falling across the outskirts of Smoke City. Over the suburbs and shopping centres it glided. It lapped over a pale stone wall, became briefly tangled in a wood of blackish trees, and struggled out again. Its movement had changed. It no longer glided. Now it seemed to be . . . *crawling*.

It crawled across a white sweep of what might have been gravel but was actually the skulls of thousands of tiny animals. It seeped through gratings into cellars, swirled round sunken gardens, and rose like a liquid up pillars. It oozed into windows and down the throats of gargoyles, chased a last golden gleam up to a weathercock in the shape of a skeleton playing an electric guitar –

Playing a *what*?

All right, all right. We are talking Castle Bones. Castle Bones, the world's greatest Feedback Metal recording studio. OK? On we go.

From a low building beside the main castle there came sounds. There was the rumble of iron wheels on gravel, the clop of hooves, the jingle of harness. A scream of whinnying. And out of the stable yard (for that was what the buildings were) there hurtled a black coach. Four black stallions foamed at the traces. On the box a coachman crouched snarling, his teeth weirdly pointed in the starlight. Down the drive they thundered. Right down the lane they turned. At the major road they gave way. The coachman extended his left hand to signify that he intended to manoeuvre. Down the Great East Road they galloped as if the very hounds of hell were after them.

As they passed the Welcome Crash services, a long, pale hand lifted the black curtain that hid the interior of the coach from the vulgar view.

'Aye, run, me dark lovelies!' roared the coachman. 'Ride to the Gates of Hell, that is to say, the Costa de Lott Estate and Golf Course for the startlingly rich!'

Behind its locked gates, Castle Bones sprawled bloated and spiky under a fingernail of moon. Nothing stirred.

Except, high in the West Wing, a window. A window with a design of iron butterflies and a catch that by the sound of it was badly in need of oiling. A window that creaked open, so that . . . *Something* . . . could look down the pale drive.

A chilly peace flowed in. And something that might have been a voice said, 'Cooooool.'

Except that there was nothing in Castle Bones. Nothing, and no one.

No one alive, anyway.

Cooooool.

1

Ladies and gentlemen, boyz'n'girls, welcome. Welcome aboard the Sandwich Supper Moonlight Tour of the Costa de Lott Estate, viewing the Homes of the Famous. Off we go! Recline in your seats, turn up the aircon of this state-of-the-art Rubaneka luxury coach, tuck into a delicious cheese sandwich mmmmm and soak up Celebridee World. Note to your left and right the high gateposts from which swing the steel gates that protect this exclusive estate. Now we are inside, look about you. Over to the right you will see men blundering around with machinery on their heads. These are Night Vision Business Golfers whose busy schedule does not permit daytime sport. And to the left, nestling among their amazingly expensive bushes, you will catch fleeting glimpses of the Houses of the Famous. Note the blazing lights and the air heavy with the perfume of ylang-ylang and imported barbecue fuels. On your left, Frou Frou Lodge, new home of Hector Vector, fourteen-year-old Minchester Unified miracle striker. Yes, madam, fourteen years old, one million per week, remarkable indeed, I said remarkable indeed, which you would have heard if you didn't have your fingers in your ears. That noise? Yes, it is indeed a very large noise —

KAJEEEEERRRRR

I said a very large noise

HOWWWWWWEEEYYYNNGGG

SKREEEE, went the brakes of the bus

— and also, ladies and gentlemen, we like totally object to carriages drawn by night-black horses driven by dwarfish coachmen who ignore the Highway Code and make . . . rude signs *at bus drivers only doing their job. This here driveway, where the coach and horses has just thundered in, belongs to*

GRAAAARNGGG

Eric Thrashmettle, who seems to be

JUNGA JUNGA JUNGA REEEE

I said practising, *madam. As everyone knows, Eric*

Thrashmettle is the greatest rocker the world of Feedback Metal has ever known. He and his band Death Eric have just completed a triumphant return tour and their album The Return of Death Eric *is only now sliding down the charts after six months way up there in the top five. If you listen closely you may get a sneak preview of their hot hot unreleased new album that everyone is already talking about. Open windows. Halt, driver. Silence, everyone!*

The lights go out. Silence falls, except for the crunch of carriage wheels on gravel and the munch of tourist jaws on cheese sandwiches. The black carriage rolls down the drive. The coachman lurches down from the box and opens the door.

Ladies and gentlemen, boyz'n'girls, look at that. The front door's opening and there are . . . oh, the Thrashmettle kids. The girl would be Lulubelle Flower Fairy Thrashmettle, twelve, and the boy would be Living Buddha Thrashmettle, eleven, and here comes Eric in person, falling slightly down the steps, you see that, greeting his guest in the carriage. Turn on the spotlights, driver. Ladies and gentlemen, we can now share this private moment as the Thrashmettle family greets a visitor . . . Hang on a minute . . . Reverse. Get out of here, driver. Oh dear . . . There goes the windscreen . . . Quick, put your foot down. We are sooo outa here . . .

*

From the doorstep of the Thrashmettle family home the Thrashmettle children watched the tour bus limp away. Its spotlights had been smashed. Several of its windows were broken, and dense white smoke belched from its exhaust pipe. The Thrashmettle children were fed up with tour buses. There were about five a night nowadays, all with spotlights. 'Good throwing, Enid,' they said.

'All in a day's work,' said a huge, beautiful woman in a print dress. Her name was Enid Bracegirdle, and she was Death Eric's main roadie, which means bodyguard, minder, fixer, all-round good egg, thrower of bricks at buses and best friend. 'Too many buses,' she said.

The bus sideswiped a tree. Three men with cameras fell out of its branches and limped away at top speed. 'And paparazzi,' said Enid.

The coachman slid down from the box of the black carriage, bowed deeply to the little party on the front steps, and opened the door. A tall woman with black hair put out a dragonskin boot and stepped into the gravel.

'Good evening, Gothalinda,' said Buddy politely.

'Good evening, Gothalinda,' said Lou, likewise.

'Mornink, evenink, who knows any more?' said

Gothalinda, walking over to them and patting their cheeks with her slender, cold fingers.

'Come in and have a cup of er,' said Eric. His hair was dyed purple today, tangled in a pair of round blue spectacles.

'He means tea,' said Living Buddha, who preferred to be known as Buddy. Not that he had anything against living buddhas. It was just that he was pretty sure he wasn't one.

'Or something fizzy,' said Lulubelle Flower Fairy, who preferred to be known as Lou. Not that she had anything against Lulubelles or Flower Fairies. It was just that while she had never seen a Flower Fairy, she was pretty sure she wasn't one.

'Yeah, whatever,' said Eric. 'Someone take the horses round the back and give them some, er, oil.'

'Hay,' said Enid, dusting brick dust off her hands.

'Hey wha?' said Eric.

'Dried grass,' said Enid. 'Horses eat it. Let's all go inside and I'll get the tea.'

Eric led the way into one of the Thrashmettles' many sitting rooms and gestured to an enormous sofa. 'Um. Siddown.'

Gothalinda sat. She turned her face on Lou. Her lips were amazingly red, her skin amazingly white, her teeth amazingly sharp. 'I *love* little childrens,' she said. 'Come and sit by me.'

The children rather liked Gothalinda too. True, she looked at you like a hungry person looking at a cheeseburger. But her recording studio at Castle Bones was like a second home to them and they had known her since they were tiny. So they sat down on the huge sofa with her, close enough for politeness but far enough away for safety, while Enid and some assistant roadies brought in tea and a jug of something deep, deep red.

Gothalinda gestured towards the jug. 'Vot is this?'

'Ribena.'

'Yes, please,' said Gothalinda, though Lou thought she saw a look of disappointment cross the pale face. Enid poured.

'How's the bat?' said Eric.

'Ve haf many bats at Castle Bones,' said Gothalinda.

'It was small and like black.'

'Ah,' said Gothalinda. 'Wery vell, I think. Also the yew trees are healthy and the Serpents of Darkness slither undimmed. How is the new album cominkk?'

'The band,' said Enid, 'is taking some time out.'

'Resting,' said Eric, lying down on the sofa and going to sleep.

'Forever?' said Gothalinda wistfully.

Eric emitted a long, peaceful snore.

'Nah,' said Enid. 'Only Eric is getting some material together, and Fingers Trubshaw (bass) and Kenyatta McClatter (drums) are like looking after their other interests. Fingers has got this lawncare company and Kenyatta has a fish-frying business. They are a bit tired of music. Too noisy, at their age. But we are hoping to go into the studio any month now. If we can find them.'

'Zat right?' said Eric, waking up.

'That's what you told the record company.'

'And,' said Buddy, 'probably they will want to record this album at Castle Bones, as usual.'

Gothalinda turned upon him her sweet, sharp smile. 'If only,' she said.

'If only wha?' said Lou.

Gothalinda looked rueful. 'I am afraid I have dropped in to tell you that Castle Bones is no more.'

'Like, someone nicked it?' said Eric.

Enid frowned. This was a business meeting, and as usual Eric was missing the point. 'Start at the beginning, Gotha,' she said. 'Tell it like it is.'

'Sank you,' said Gothalinda, setting her hands in her red velvet lap. 'Vell. A lonk time ago, we took over the studio at Castle Bones. Efferyone used it. Spinal Tap, Motley Crue, Blek Sabbat –'

'Who?' said Eric.

'– efferyone. But now is different. Now effery geezer who has a guitar can schtick it in his computer und bingo! Album-quality recording.'

'It's not the same,' said Buddy soothingly.

'You know that and I know that,' said Gothalinda. 'But you try tellink Radio Vun.' She made a complicated curse gesture. 'So anyvay. The maintenance is a killer. The staff problems, vell, you try employink an engineer that is a werewolf. Plus there is a curse obviously and a ghost, and at my age you can't be doing with curses.'

'You don't look very old to me,' said Lou.

'I'm seven hundred and twenty-vun,' said Gothalinda. 'I've had enough. The pressure got to me. I slid back into . . . vell.'

'You haven't been drinking blood again?' said Enid.

'I'm not proud of it. I need help. I must take some time off and go into revamp.'

'Re what?'

'Like rehab, but for the vampire community. Anyway, I am looking for someone to live in Castle Bones.'

'You're *what?*' said the children, for whom Castle Bones was a much-loved fixed point in rather random lives.

'I'm retiring,' said Gothalinda. 'After revamp I plan to bury myself in the country. Someone wants to buy Castle Bones. A fat man in a vaistcoat. He says it vill make a very loffly country club mit eighteen-hole golf course and fishing. He says he can deal with the Ghost.'

There was a silence. 'Castle Bones Country Club?' said Lou. 'I don't get it.'

'The Castle Bones where Death Eric recorded their legendary *Return of Death Eric* album?' said Buddy. 'A *golf* club? No *way.*'

Gothalinda spread her delicate white hands in a gesture of hopelessness. 'Vay,' she said.

'I'll buy it,' said Eric from the sofa.

'Wha,' said everybody except Gothalinda, who was suddenly (thought Lou) looking just the smallest bit triumphant.

Eric sat up and fell off the sofa. 'There is a bat there,' he said as Enid picked him up off the floor.

'Where?' said everyone, looking wildly round the room.

'At Castle Bones. His name is Norbert and he is very, very like me. Except for the ears, and the wings, and of course he can't play guitar because of webbed fingers, plus he is a bat not a person. But I really like that bat and I will defend his home against any like pig or swine who wants to turn it into a golf ball.'

'Club.'

'Exactly. Plus I have never met a ghost and the kids might like it.'

Enid's face looked like a huge rugged landscape over which clouds were forming. 'I'll call Stiggy,' she said, in a voice that was not at all convinced.

'Who?'

'Stiggy is your latest manager.' The clouds were thick and dark, with thunder in them.

'Oh. Yeah.'

'Enid,' said Lou. 'We like Castle Bones. My pet snakes will love it, the rats, you know. And there are too many tourist buses and nosy parkers round here nowadays, you said so yourself. This is a good idea at a very good time.'

'You do not understand,' said Enid.

'Vot is your problem, Enid?' said Gothalinda.

'Problem?' said Enid, battering buttons on her mobile phone. 'Castle Bones is all very well. But can the band afford it? I mean, the record company is going, Where's the album? And, You need a new look, and things are tight. Plus ghosts. I dunno.'

'We have never met a ghost,' said Buddy.

'They may be extremely interesting,' said Lou.

'Yeah,' said Enid, sighing a bit, because this was rock and roll, after all. 'If you say so. No problem. Just callin' up the management. Stiggy?' Pause, listening. 'Yeah. See you in five.' She turned to the assembled company. 'He's in the chopper,' she said. 'He'll be here any minute.'

Sure enough, rotors clattered, the lights on the Dunravin helipad lanced brilliantly into the sky, a red chopper swooped out of the night, and a figure in a dark suit jumped out and jogged towards the house.

'Bet he pats us on the head,' said Lou.

'And chucks us under the chin,' said Buddy. 'And tells us that tourist buses are good publicity.'

The door burst open. In trotted the suit. On top of it were short black hair, long white teeth, and a round brown face. On the bottom of it were shiny black shoes with little gold snaffle bits on. All around it was a cloud of Mon Skunque Cologne for Men.

'Well hello hello hell*o*,' cried the suit, trotting across the room, patting Lou on the head, chucking Buddy under the chin, and shaking hands warmly with everyone else except Eric, who had vanished. 'Three tourist buses in the drive. *Great* publicity. Eric here?'

'Not here,' said a voice from under the sofa.

'Cool. Fine. Wonderful. Super. Marvellous,' said Stiggy, shooshing the magic of his personality round the room like fire-extinguisher foam. 'And it's Draculetta, innit?'

'Gothalinda,' said Lou.

'Like I said, Gothalinda. And how *is* it over in Skull Manor?'

'Castle Bones,' said Buddy.

'Whatever. Dead unhygienic, if you ask me.'

Gothalinda's manner had become extra chilly. 'I do not remember asking you anythink.'

'Brilliant. Super. Cool. Fine,' said Stiggy.

'Gothalinda wants Eric to buy Castle Bones,' said Enid.

'So do we,' said Buddy and Lou.

Stiggy's beaming smile did not falter. 'Wild.

Excellent. Cool. That old dump? She must be out of her mind.'

'Stiggy?' said Eric's voice from under the sofa. 'Zat you?'

'Certainly is,' said Stiggy, wriggling with delight at the idea.

'You're fired,' said the voice from under the sofa.

There was a silence, broken only by the click of Stiggy's jaw falling open.

'The door is on your left,' said Lou.

'The round thing on the right-hand side is the handle,' said Buddy.

'Ahahahaha,' said Stiggy. 'Only joking. Lovely, I mean super, marvellous, cool. Castle Bones, eh? How much?'

'Give her what she wants,' said the voice under the sofa.

'But . . .' said Enid.

The record company wanted a new album and a new look. But Death Eric was old, not new. The band were happy mowing lawns and frying fish. And Castle Bones was old too. And very, very expensive . . .

'It will be a big help with the new album,' said

Eric. 'I will like record it at Castle Bones with the help of, er . . .'

'The engineer?' ventured Enid.

'Obviously. But no.'

'The band?'

'Obviously. But no.'

'The, er, *ghost*?'

'Ghost, maybe. But definitely bat. With the help of the bat. Which is called like Norbert.'

'Are you sure?' Enid asked.

'Bats do not speak French,' said Eric knowledgeably. 'Norbert is a French name. So he will not know whether or not he is called Norbert. So it is his name, as likely as not.'

'Not sure about Norbert the bat. Sure about buying Castle Bones.'

'Oh. Yeah.'

'Well!' said Stiggy. 'So that's settled, then. Happy, Morticia?'

'Gothalinda. Yes.' Her black eyes rested on Stiggy's jugular vein.

'Great. Super. Fabulous. Wowsie –'

'*Wowsie?*' said Lou and Buddy together.

'– so Enid, organize the move, will you?'

'Er,' said Buddy. 'I thought you were fired, Stiggy.'

'Yes,' said Lou. 'What do you reckon, Enid?'

Enid eyed Stiggy coldly. She had never met a manager who could manage better than her, except the ones she fell in love with, and Stiggy was definitely not one of those.

'Stiggy,' she said. 'On yer bike.'

'I haven't got one.'

Enid started to roll up the sleeves of her print dress, revealing brawny forearms heavily tattooed. 'Run off to bed, children,' she said. 'The evening is about to get nasty.'

The door slammed. A whiff of Mon Skunque hung in the room, and expensive loafers sprinted on the gravel outside, pounding towards the tall timber.

Stiggy was gone. Death Eric was without a manager.

'So,' said Gothalinda. 'Ve haf a deal.'

'Yeah,' said Eric.

'It vill cost you lots, but that is OK,' said Gothalinda. 'Also, I vill send you a portrait of me for the Long Long Gallery. You vill like it.'

'Of course we will,' said Lou.

Moving house is a complicated process. Moving Rock and Roll Mansions is a lot worse. Lou and

Buddy sat in the chairs behind their desks, directing the roadies.

'Careful with that snake!' cried Lou.

'Ggah,' said the roadie from inside the coils.

'Steady with that bear!' cried Buddy.

'Mmmph!' said the roadie from inside a rather crushing hug.

Staff and animals tottered downstairs. Buddy and Lou went to help Enid, who was in Eric's room. They could hear their father's voice as they went up the stairs. He sounded anxious.

'Got my guitar?' he said.

'Yes, Eric.'

'Got my boot?'

'Yes, Eric.'

'Got my other boot?'

'Yes, Eric. Got everything, Eric.'

'Everything? What about the new album?'

'We have not yet recorded the new album,' said Enid. 'Or even written it.'

'Do you think you ever will?' said Lou.

'Of course they will,' said Buddy. 'We will make sure of that.'

'I done it already,' said Eric.

'Stone me,' said Enid. 'Show us, then.'

There was a pause, with the sound of someone rummaging through shoeboxes full of paper.

'It's in here somewhere.'

'The record company will not half be relieved,' said Enid. 'They've been worrying.'

More rustling.

Then Enid said, 'Is that *it*?'

Lou and Buddy went in at the door. The walls were purple, the curtains black with little silver bats on them. Eric was holding up a single sheet of paper with big writing on it. LIVE, said the writing.

'Yeah,' said Eric, apparently nettled. 'Live album. What's wrong with that?'

'Great,' said Enid. 'Only . . . well, I think the record company hoped you might be . . . a bit further along with it.'

'Stiggy liked it.'

'Tell me one thing Stiggy did not like.'

There was a pause.

'They want that new album,' said Enid. 'And the new look. Soon.'

'Hmm,' said Lou, 'I wonder where the band is?'

'We'll ring 'em up,' said Lou.

Buddy rang.

'You have reached the offices of Green Fingers

Trubshaw. Lawncare Specialists,' said the answering machine. 'We are out caring for lawns. Leave a message.' There was about five minutes of rustic heyho music, then a beep.

'Come to Castle Bones,' said Buddy. 'You're making an album.'

Kenyatta's answering machine was different, obviously. 'I am telling you and I am not lying that I am off in my van and probably frying,' said the voice. 'If you're a lovely lady and all alone, please leave a message after the tone. If you are not then go away and I'll maybe catch you another day. Or maybe not. Irie. Beep.'

'Hurry to Castle Bones,' said Buddy. 'Album time.'

And that, for the moment, was all they could do.

Normally, the Thrashmettle children would have gone to the Blue Room to play calming music, which would have put them in a good frame of mind for deciding what to do next. But Dunravin was in a ferment of packing, needing something at the bottom of a suitcase, unpacking, finding it and repacking. So they sat in the kitchen in a state of some anxiety. Last time there had been no manager, no album and no band, the credit cards had stopped working. Lou and Buddy were very close, almost telepathic at times.

'We are talented musicians,' said Lou. 'And keen readers of lovely new books. Which cost money.'

'Brought up in luxury,' said Buddy. 'Surrounded by the finest scientific instruments with which we do important experiments. Which happen to be rather expensive.'

'And we need to keep things that way,' said Lou.

'So we will look out for ourselves and do the best for our parents and entourage.'

'True.'

They shook hands. Then they went outside and had a look round. Eventually, they found Enid.

'Oi,' they said. 'Take us to Castle Bones.'

'Manners,' said Enid. 'Say bleedin' please.'

'Bleedin' please take us to Castle Bones,' said Buddy and Lou.

'Course,' said Enid. 'Hop in.'

Into a limo they hopped. Off they went.

Many people have tried to describe Castle Bones. Few have had any success. Most people say it is big, though some say very big, and others gigantic.

Tarpon's *Guide to Great Buildings* says it is a fine example of the Norman-Gothic-Baroque-Rococo-Lotterywinner School of architecture. This is all very well, but it leaves out one of Castle Bones' main ingredients, i.e. Menace.

So let us try starting from scratch.

Castle Bones was built in the Middle Ages, and improved about a hundred and fifty years ago by a Mr Ephraim Muckybrass, who had made a lot of money digging up the lost treasure of a South American tribe whose name had long been forgotten, even by them. He had bought a large section of the valley of the River Dusk, on the outskirts of the village of Honeyborough, which would later grow into Smoke City. There he had started mending and extending the already enormous castle. The building had soaked up money sullenly and yelled for more.

What Ephraim Muckybrass did not know was that as well as money, he had also poured into the house the curse he had brought back with the treasure. The South American tribe had kept such curses at bay with human sacrifice. But human sacrifices are frowned on nowadays. So the curse did its work, twisting trees, thickening shadows, and making animals that were normally warm and furry cold and slimy. Obviously in its home country the curse would have flattened the castle and returned it to jungle. But it had fallen victim to Distance Dilution, which is the natural force that makes the basketwork donkey that looked so sweet on your holiday in Spain look so horrible when you stick it to your bedroom wall.

So Castle Bones was very big, very dark, very weird, and (thanks to the curse) very Menacing.

It was this that had attracted Dave Krang.

In the far-off infancy of metal music, Aluminium Dave Krang had been very, very famous. His records had sold in millions, his concerts had caused gridlock in the capital cities of the world, and his personal life had attracted many X certificates and been banned in Guildford. Then in 1966 Dave Krang had decided to turn Castle Bones into the greatest recording studio the world had seen.

The River Dusk was diverted and dammed into the Cooling Lake for the Transformer. The many dismal grottoes were converted into Echo Chambers. The wine cellars were filled with glowing cities of valves. Enormous mixing boards were installed in the crypts, and studios soundproofed with sheet lead, and a marimba made of human bones. He cut two award-winning albums. Then one day the Big Transformer blew one of its barrel-sized fuses, and Krang, a keen skin-diver, plunged into the lake to do repairs.

And was never seen again.

Well, not until . . .

But we will come to this later.

Castle Bones was bought by many owners, the last of whom was Gothalinda Bathory from the Dark Central Mountains, who was used to castles with curses on them, having lived in them since her birth in 1287. And now Gothalinda had sold out to Eric Thrashmettle.

One of whose stretch Cadillacs was at that very moment heading through the suburbs of Smoke City, with Lou and Buddy in the back seat and Enid in the front.

So there you are. Up to date.

As the limo drew close to the valley of the River Dusk, the houses of Smoke City took on a stunted look. Large black birds flew overhead. The road began to slope downward. Now the houses had no glass in the windows. Further along, the houses had actually fallen down. And suddenly a wall stretched across the world ahead, tall and blackish. On the far side of the wall were visible the tops of dark trees, shuddering in a small, cold wind.

'Oh, I'm so excited!' cried Lou, clapping her hands.

'Peace at last,' said Buddy. 'No tour coaches here.'

'Except that one,' said Lou, pointing at something that had once been a coach and was now in a ditch, having apparently been burnt out.

'And here we are,' said Enid brightly, hauling the limo into a handbrake turn in front of a pair of gates tastefully decorated with henbane and deadly nightshade in wrought iron. 'Ooer.'

The lodge door had opened, and a tall, thin man with a bald head limped out. He was so stooped that every time he took a step his knees hit his chin, clacking his teeth together.

'New young masters, clonk,' he mumbled, knuckling his forehead. He shoved the gates open with a tearing squeak.

'Get some oil on them hinges, Granpa!' cried Enid, spraying him with gravel as she whacked her size twelve on the throttle.

The drive snaked down through thick black groves of yews. There was a rickety bridge over a gorge in whose bed a river thundered. And there in front of them, occupying most of the top of a medium-sized plateau, lay Castle Bones. Night was falling, and all the windows were dark –

'Hey!' said Buddy, glancing at his Rolex. 'It's only lunchtime.'

Correction. Night was not yet falling, but all the windows were dark except for one, halfway along the West Wing.

'I'm starving,' said Lou.

'Me too,' said Buddy.

Enid parked the limo in the stable yard. The children walked round to the front of the castle, across a sweep covered not with gravel but with the skulls of small animals.

'Ours at last!' said Lou, opening the front door. 'Coo-ee,' she cried. 'Anyone in?'

'Wooo,' cried an owl in the woods.

'Dear old Hall of Columns,' said Buddy.

And there they were, the columns, white as bones, stretching away into the shadows. A toad was hauling itself towards the fountain in the middle. Buddy stooped to give it a helping hand.

'Buddy,' said Lou, gripping her brother's arm. 'What's that?'

Far away, beyond many columns, the shadows lay thick and dark. Where they lay darkest was a dull yellow spark, bobbing and lurching.

There was a moment's complete silence, broken only by the drip of water, the chitter of bats, and the scuttle of claws on slimy stones. All right, not complete silence then. But as close to it as you got at Castle Bones.

'Hoi!' cried Lou. *Hoi, hoi, hoi,* cried the echoes. 'Who's that?'

'I are I,' creaked an ancient rustic voice. 'Mrs Drear. I am the housekeeper what lurks hereabouts. And 'oo might you be, my poppet?'

'Our name is Thrashmettle,' said Lou.

'Ah!' cried Mrs Drear. 'I done read about you in *Famerse!* magazine. You do be liddle Lulubelle Flower Fairy and this year will be your liddle brother Livin' Buddha.'

'We are Lou and Buddy,' said Lou crisply. 'Make a note of that.' Her eyes were getting accustomed to the shadows. She saw a little bent lady in a long black dress, holding a lantern over her head. The light of the lantern gleamed on dusty grey curls and a maze of wrinkles on an ancient face. 'Now then,' said Lou, 'where's the kitchen? We're hungry.'

'Follow me,' said Mrs Drear. 'Heh, heh.'

'Is something funny?' said Lou.

'In Castle Bones we larfs so as not to weep,' said Mrs Drear.

She hobbled off among the columns. As she faded into the twilight she seemed to trip on something. The lantern hit the stone floor and went out. Darkness swept in among the columns.

'Oh, *really*,' said Enid's voice from the far side of the hall.

There was a click. The lights came on.

'So what was all that lantern stuff for?' said Lou.

Mrs Drear lay on the flagstones like a grounded bat. She moaned instead of answering.

'She's hurt her leg,' said Buddy. 'Let's take a look.'

'Dunna touch me gams!' cried Mrs Drear.

'Speak English,' said Buddy, examining the old lady's leg with fingers that had done a first aid course and mended several bears. 'No bones broken . . . oi!'

'Wha,' said Lou.

'Wha,' said Enid, who was now standing by.

'Me footses!' cried Mrs Drear.

'Yes,' said Buddy. 'Look, though.' He pulled up the rusty black skirt.

'Me legses!' cried Mrs Drear. 'Me modesty!'

'There's nothing wrong with your leg,' said Buddy. 'But this is a weird shoe. There is a pocket in the sole, and you put this in it.' He held up a brick.

'Me brickses!' cried Mrs Drear, but Lou could tell she was losing heart.

'So your limp is because you are walking with one ordinary shoe and one shoe with a brick in a special pocket in its sole.'

Lou had been frowning at Mrs Drear's silver curls. Now she bent, grasped a handful, and tugged. The curls came away.

'Me curlses!' said Mrs Drear, but she had given up now, and there was no more expression in her voice than if she had been saying she was off down the shops for a pound of rat poison.

'Tell all,' said Enid grimly.

'Oi are the 'ousekeeperr,' said Mrs Drear. 'Oi bin year woman and girrl –'

'No you haven't,' said Lou. 'We were here to record Dad's last album and we never saw you.'

Enid was peering at her. 'I know you,' she said. 'Oh?'

'You were Libby Squid in *Westenders*! Wow!'

'*Westenders*?' said Lou, who like her brother was too busy playing music to watch much TV.

'You were quite good,' said Enid, shaking her head wonderingly. 'Murdered by Roxy Dave the wicked landlord of the King Kong.'

'Oo,' said Mrs Drear, standing up straight and running her fingers through what now seemed to be her flowing blonde hair. 'So glad you liked it. Do you want my autograph, darling?'

'Not much,' said Enid. 'What are you doing here?'

'What is a girl *supposed* to do when she was the Face of Smoke City and suddenly there is no work any more? Gothalinda gave me a job, a cameo really, as the Weird Housekeeper, bless her. And now I suppose you'll give me the sack.'

'Yes,' said Lou. 'Unless you take us to the kitchen right now because we are *starving*.'

'And lay off the Weird Housekeeper stuff.'

'Arr my mommets, my liddle poppets –'

'*Libby!*'

'Sorry, darling, slipped into character.'

The electric lights dimmed, and a cold draught

flowed through the Hall of Columns. A mighty peal of laughter rattled among the pillars.

'What was *that*?' said Lou, whose hair was standing on end.

'Aarr my liddle –'

'Oh, forget it,' said Buddy.

'Sorry,' said Libby. 'Force of habit. That was the Ghost.'

'There really is a ghost?' said Lou. 'I thought that was just Gothalinda being, you know, a salesperson.'

'You don't seem very frightened,' said Libby.

'Ghosts are dead,' said Buddy. 'What's dead can't hurt you.'

'Not like black mambas,' said Lou. 'Or grizzly bears.'

'Has this ghost ever bitten anyone?'

'Nobody much.'

'Much?'

'All right, nobody. He's just a bit, well, terrifying.'

'Yeah,' said Buddy, ironically.

'Oo,' said Lou, sarcastically.

'Lunch,' said Buddy.

'Now,' said Lou.

Off they went.

*

The kitchens at Castle Bones were very big and very old. No health and safety inspector had ever inspected them and lived. There was an open fire with a spit. There was an enormous black iron stove, and sinks of slimy green stone.

'Welcome to the kitchens, featuring the Great Cauldron of Castle Bones,' said Libby Squid, waving a hand at the fireplace. 'It's, um, like an ancient jacuzzi. The cauldron is six metres across and always kept full of . . . water.'

'Fascinating,' said Enid politely. 'What's for lunch?'

Ms Squid produced some only slightly burnt pizza and salad.

'We'll soon fix up the kitchen,' said Lou afterwards.

'Stainless-steel counters,' said Buddy. 'Walk-in freezer. Smoothie machines, all that.'

'Quite. Now,' said Lou, who was slightly overcome by the heat of the black iron range, which showed signs of turning red, 'I fancy a swim.'

'Me too!' cried Buddy.

'Bit soon after lunch, isn't it?' said Libby.

'It is Enid's job to rescue us.'

'Course it is,' said Enid stoutly.

Stripping to their Calvin Kleins, the Thrash-mettle children leaped into the Great Cauldron and splashed happily.

Somewhere in the distant reaches of the enormous building a clock struck two.

'Urgh!' cried Lou.

'Yuk!' cried Buddy.

For the water in which they were swimming was not clear any more. It had turned a deep, deep red, darker than letterboxes, lighter than maroon, roughly the colour of . . .

'Blood!' cried Lou.

'Eur!' cried Buddy.

Out they climbed, and cast themselves red and dripping into the great sink, where Enid hosed them off under the warmish tap.

'How disgusting,' said Lou.

'Could have been worse,' said Buddy, scrubbing.

In a family whose father eats animals on stage, including live bats and your hamster if he can get his hands on it, the odd bath in blood is all part of the day's rich pageant.

Not everyone at Castle Bones knew this, of course.

In a little room somewhere behind the East

Battlements, Something sat in an ancient carved chair and listened to the cries of horror and dismay echoing up the kitchen chimney. It writhed a bit. And down the Long Long Gallery and the Double Stairs and the enormous kitchen chimney there echoed peal upon peal of demoniac laughter.

Or would have echoed. Had it not been drowned by the roar of engines and the crunch of wheels on stoats' skulls as a great fleet of limos, Trannies, Hummers and artics pulled into the drive.

The main Thrashmettle entourage had arrived at Castle Bones.

2

The Thrashmettles settled in quickly. Roadies can live just about anywhere. Eric had no idea where he was most of the time. And Buddy and Lou liked a project.

There were plenty of projects at Castle Bones. Naturally, Buddy had made a list:

(1) Find out why the water in the Great Cauldron turns to blood on the stroke of 2 p.m.
(2) Find out more about the Ghost.

(3) Get the band back together to play on the new album.

(4) Make sure they get a new look so the record company pays up and everyone can afford to go on living at the castle.

(5) That's it.

These were not in order of importance, of course. Anyone could fill a cauldron with blood, but only Death Eric could make a Death Eric album.

'So,' said Lou, as she and Buddy had a spaghetti lunch (cooked by Cookie, the band cook) next day in the Hall of Columns with Enid and Sid the Soothsayer, Eric's useless fortune-teller. 'Step One is to get the band back together. Fingers Trubshaw (bass) has not rung back. Nor has Kenyatta McClatter (drums). I wonder where they are.'

'I will haruspicate,' said Sid the Soothsayer.

'You will wha?'

'Haruspication is telling the future through the entrails of animals,' said Buddy, showing off quite a lot.

'I been on a course,' said Sid the Soothsayer. '*Vegan* haruspication. You do it with like spaghetti.' He stirred his plateful. 'Anyway. Yeah. Kenyatta and Fingers are together. They are on a tropical island. I see a full moon –'

'It says here,' said Enid, who had been reading *Who?!* magazine, 'that Fingers is at a flower show and Kenyatta is taking fish-frying lessons somewhere.'

'Like I said, flowers and fish,' said Sid.

A ghostly snigger sounded in the shadows of the hall.

'What was that?' said Lou.

'Drains,' said Sid.

'You wish,' said Libby Squid, looking nervously about her. 'It's nearly two o'clock.'

'Oh,' said Buddy, brightening. 'Right. Shall we go?'

'That thing with the cauldron won't happen again,' said Sid.

They trooped into the kitchen. Fitters were installing juicers and tofu engines. But the huge fireplace was as usual, with the Great Cauldron hanging from its iron crane over a fire of fat yew logs from the castle woods.

Tick, said the huge clock. Tock. BONG.

'Two o'clock,' said Sid. BONG. 'Nothing. Told ya.'

As he said 'ya', something troubled the shining

surface of the water in the cauldron. Ripples ran across it. It bubbled, then foamed. The foam turned pink, then red.

'Nice one, Sid,' said Enid.

For the water in the cauldron had quite definitely turned to blood.

There was a frozen silence. Down the chimney there came a truly fearsome noise: a long, bubbling cackle, full of horror and triumph.

Libby Squid fainted with a clunk. Lou did not much like it either. But Buddy stuck his head up the chimney.

'Oi!' he shouted. 'Hyena face! We wanna swim and we do not like swimming in blood! Got it?'

'Manners,' said Enid.

'Never mind manners,' said Buddy. 'This is our house, and I do not see why we should put up with silly old ghosts making life diff– What is it?'

'Aren't you *frightened*?' said Libby.

'Ghosts are like bullies,' said Buddy. 'Show fear and you've had it. Don't laugh!' he yelled up the chimney, where the cackle was beginning again.

But the cackle got louder –

and was drowned by the sound of mighty engines in the drive. Everyone piled out of the castle. The stoat skulls were suddenly crowded with vehicles. Buddy took one look and stopped. The crowd went past him, except Lou, who had stopped too.

'It's Mum,' said Lou gloomily.

'Oh,' said Buddy without enthusiasm. Slightly to his horror, he found he was holding his sister's hand.

Wave Thrashmettle, mother of Lou and Buddy and wife of Eric, was a woman of sudden and violent enthusiasms. And the things she was enthusiastic about were often deeply embarrassing. Somewhere in the house the ghostly laughter continued, peal on echoing peal. But since the arrival of Wave Thrashmettle there were worse things than ghosts at Castle Bones.

Beyond the line of big people there was now a babble of conversation, much of it in a foreign language. And a voice.

'Where arrr my LEETLE ONES?' it cried.

'It's Mum,' said Lou. 'Putting on a weird accent.'

'Doesn't sound like she's into yoga any more,' said Buddy.

The crowd parted. A figure streaked through: a figure dressed in a red felt shirt, soft black-leather boots, an embroidered jerkin and a black hat with a band of silver coins.

'Slobodna brodnye!' cried the figure. 'Lulubelski and Budvar! Dollinks!'

'Hello, Mum,' said Lou and Buddy gloomily.

'Come!' cried their mother, her eyes gleaming in an alarming manner. 'Let us have many pies! The music of the ood!'

'Ood?' said Buddy.

A fearsome clanging noise broke out behind Wave. A small man in a fur hat rocketed into the air above the crowd, arms folded, boots kicking out in all directions.

'Yes, the wonderful ood, breath and hamstring of the motherland, says the great Honganian poet Splatchov!'

'Gesundheit,' said Buddy politely, watching the small man finish rocketing and start to plummet.

'So you are back,' said Lou, shaking her head to clear it.

'Indeed!' cried Wave. 'Me and the Honganian Folk Orchestra, the planet's leading players of Whirl Music. Spiggy the manager –'

'Ex-manager.'

'Whatever, said the band needed a New Look!

And I have brought one! Yes, we have come to help your father make his new ground-breaking Whirl Music album! Now! Let our blood sing with merriness!'

'Quite,' said Buddy. The ood ensemble was making a noise like a motorway pile-up in a greenhouse complex. 'But last time we saw you, you were into yoga.'

'Yoga is so *last week*!' cried Wave. 'Life is for living! Bring sour milk and heavy pies!'

Twenty minutes later, the Thrashmettle family and entourage were sitting at the long table in the Banqueting Hall. From the carved rafters, hideous demon faces glared down. From the lower parts of the long table, hideous roadie faces glared back.

A Honganian lady began to bang pies down on the table. The pies were followed by large earthenware jugs.

'Eat! Eat!' cried Wave embarrassingly, pouring herself a glass of something white and lumpy.

'We've already had spaghetti,' said Lou. 'Cookie made it.'

'Any beans?' said Eric.

'Just pies,' said Wave.

'A pie without beans is like a night without moon-light,' said Eric.

'Wha,' said the whole table, who had never before heard him talk in proverbs.

'Hoot,' said Flatpick the budgie, who since his arrival at Castle Bones had decided chirruping was not dignified.

'That looks delicious,' said Sid the Soothsayer, eyeing his pie.

'Ugh,' said a roadie, biting into his.

'Leave them,' said Buddy. 'C'mon, Lou.'

They walked out of the castle and up to a Gothic cottage on a nearby crag.

'This is not the New Look the record company wanted,' said Lou. 'More like a load of rubbish.'

'Yep,' said Buddy. 'We've got to get rid of them. Any ideas?'

'Not yet,' said Lou. She patted the special pocket in her blazer in which she kept her copy of *Tales from the Brothers Grime*, that small, leather-bound fountain (she reckoned) of all wisdom. 'But the Brothers will have an answer.'

'Yeah, right,' said Buddy.

There was a piano in the cottage, and Lou's cello, propped by roadies against a hippo's skull. They played Stork's Music for Rainy Lunchtime; not that it was raining, but at Castle Bones it always seemed to be about to. Afterwards they felt refreshed, as usual.

'Let's have an explore,' said Lou.

They went down a winding path into the gorge of the Dusk, to the edge of the Transformer Lake. It was a great bowl of ground, with the lake at its base and a flat island near its upstream end. The breeze sighed unhappily in the trees.

'It's nice not to have paparazzi,' said Buddy.

'In a miserable sort of way,' said Lou.

'We'll get used to it,' said Buddy. 'What's that?'

They stopped, listening. A curious buzzing, not unlike a bee, was coming from what looked like a rabbit hole. Lou knelt and put her ear to it.

YONGZINGBINGZANGAKKABONGZ-INGZEE, said the rabbit hole in a high weird drone.

'Chanting,' said Lou.

'Rabbits don't chant,' said Buddy.

They looked around. The ground was made of a silvery sand that contrasted eerily with the yew trees. In the sand were footprints.

'A woman,' said Buddy. 'Five foot four inches tall,

walking slowly, with a bit of chewing gum stuck to the sole of her left shoe.'

'Let's go,' said Lou.

They followed the footprints down a flight of steps. At the bottom of the steps yellow light wobbled on water, and the chanting seemed louder. Buddy, in front, put out a warning arm. Lou stopped. She was glad she was close to her brother. Frankly, she was creeped out.

The children put their heads round the corner. They were looking into a cave, floored with water. Yellow light wobbled on the water, and the chanting seemed louder. At the far end was a beach. Above the beach was a boulder with a smiley face painted on it. On top of the boulder were many candles, from which the light came. And on the beach beside a pair of shoes sat a woman, cross-legged, eyes closed, chanting. The woman was Libby Squid. Candlelight was visible between her bottom and the beach.

'I was right about the chewing gum,' said Buddy.

'Wha? Chewing gum? She's actually *floating*. In mid air. By yoga.'

'Yeah. Well. It's a Meditation Cave. What else would she be doing?'

'But *floating*. That's really interesting.'

'Not to me.'

'Obviously not. But to Mum.' Lou touched the leatherbound *Brothers Grime* in its special pocket. 'Did you never hear the Tale of the Turkey and the Swallow?'

'No,' said Buddy nervously.

'There was this swallow that lived in the same barn as a turkey called Doris, who was a great nuisance. So the other turkeys got the swallow in a corner and said, "It must be lovely, migrating off to the South like that. Plus you are rather small. Have you ever thought of a bit of company on the trip? *Big* company, in case of accidents. For accidents can happen."

'"Er . . ." said the swallow.

'"Tell you what, then," said the turkeys. "You teach our Doris to migrate, and we'll make sure she looks after you and we will also save your nesting place for next year. You know," they said, "there is a lot of pressure on nesting places. Everyone is after them."

'"It's a nightmare," said the swallow.

'Then they all went to Doris. "Doris," they said. "That swallow up there thinks you're a great flyer. It'd like to show you the Warm South."

'"Oo," said Doris, for she had always known that something like this would happen one day.

'So that autumn, off they went.'

There was a silence. Lou put the book away.

'Is that it?' said Buddy.

'That's it.'

'Hmm,' said Buddy. 'I see. I think.'

HIMBOMSQUINGZINGSPLOT-TABONG, chanted Libby Squid, drifting slightly down the beach.

'Oi,' said Lou.

'ZINGZANG ouch,' said Libby, falling to earth with a bump. 'Wha?'

'Sorry,' said Lou insincerely. 'Have you met our mum?'

'No,' said Libby, still cross.

'Then you ought to,' said Lou.

'Definitely,' said Buddy, to whom his sister's plan had suddenly become clear.

As they walked back to the castle, they saw Enid on the other side of the gorge. She was with a tall man with black hair. The tall man was waving his hands and talking. Enid was nodding, looking up into his face and nodding again.

'It looks like they're taking a stroll,' said Buddy.

'Sauntering,' said Lou.

Buddy was looking grim. Enid mostly strode or ran. She had never sauntered in her life. 'Let's check her out,' he said.

They crossed the river by a small bridge with a balustrade of iron bones.

'Hi, Enid,' said Lou.

Enid stopped. She was looking very pretty and absolutely enormous, and her print dress was blowing about her exquisitely tattooed knees.

'Hi, kids,' she said. 'Er, this is Vlad.' She pointed to the tall, dark man, who smelt disgustingly of tobacco. 'He's just come from Hongania.' She made a small, bad drawing of nothing much in the sand with her size twelve. 'He's the new management. They call him Vlad the Inhaler.'

Lou was looking at Enid very closely. She was definitely blushing.

'New management?' said Buddy. 'Since when?'

The evil-smelling Vlad gave him a dark, sleepy look from the bottom of his eyes. 'Since fifteen minutes, child. Vot are you doing here?'

'This is Eric's daughter,' said Enid, definitely batting her eyelashes. 'And his son.'

Vlad swept a low bow. He was wearing a black cloak, and black jeans, and a black shirt, and a black belt with a silver skull buckle, and boots made of the skin of some sort of black lizard, and an evil-smelling cigarette. 'Charrmed,' he said.

'Yeah, well,' said Buddy, who had met smoothies before. 'Who else do you manage?'

'My interests are . . . varied,' said Vlad.

'Oo you are awful,' said Enid, with a stomach-churning giggle.

'Who?' said Lou.

'Is like a voodful of owls round here,' said Vlad. 'Vell, there was Volfie.'

'Wolfman Jack, the legendary DJ?'

'Volfgang Amadeus, insect. Mr Mozart to you.'

'Really?' said Lou.

'But of course you never heard of him,' said Vlad, blowing a large cloud of nasty smoke.

The air of Castle Bones was never exactly warm. Now, even Enid felt the temperature drop a few degrees.

'No, never,' said Buddy, for whom grade eight in keyboards was a distant but charming memory.

'Who?' said Lou, whose version of the Mozart

Cello Sonata had won her more prizes than her bedroom shelf would hold.

'Er . . .' said Enid, surfacing from her love trance and feeling the chill in the air.

'Silence, little voman,' said masterful Vlad. 'Now. Please to come back to the castle, for I have an announcement to make.'

'Oo,' said Buddy insincerely.

'How thrilling,' said Lou, likewise.

Vlad strode off. Enid hung back.

'It's just his way,' she said. 'Very masterful, these international Honganian rock and roll managers.'

'So it seems,' said Buddy.

'You will be nice to him?' said Enid.

'Maybe,' said Lou.

'Or maybe not,' said Buddy.

High in the West Wing, in a stone cell with a window but no door, Something ran a bony finger down a chromatic scale of ribs. The Something did not have eyes or ears, exactly. But it had a pretty good sense of what was going on, and it could tell that what was going on was trouble.

Thunder boomed in the heavy sky, and the clouds felt full of rain. They weren't, but they did.

The Something laughed. The castle shook a little.

Trouble?

Lovely.

The entire Death Eric entourage was gathered in the Hall of Columns. Someone had arranged some greenish spotlights and a stage. A single blue follow-spot fell on a hooded black figure walking . . . no, *gliding* . . . among the columns. The figure stepped on to the stage. With a dramatic gesture, he threw back his hood, flipped the edge of his cloak over his shoulder and threw a cigarette end into the toad pool. With another, he swept his mane of black hair out of his eyes.

'Greetings, Vlad!' chorused the Honganian Folk Orchestra, who were squatting among some columns cooking pies on a portable stove.

'Oo,' said Enid, quivering a bit as Vlad's eyes swept across her.

'Greetings, mortals,' said Vlad. 'I believe we are all here? Good –'

'No,' said Lou.

'Wha,' said Vlad, put off his stroke.

'Dad's not,' said Buddy. 'Nor's the band.'

'Oi,' said a voice from the shadows. ' 'Sme.'

Eric shuffled into view. He walked into a column, said, 'Sorry, man,' and wove onward. Enid was already moving swiftly towards him. Eric stopped and sat down in a place where there was no chair. Quick as a flash, Enid put one under him.

'Wow,' said Eric, pleasantly surprised at this rare successful standing-to-sitting experience. He belched. 'Pies,' he said. 'A pie without beans is like a night without –'

'Yes, verry interesting, as I wass saying,' said Vlad. 'Now the talent is here –'

'But not the whole band,' said Lou, doggedly.

Vlad turned his eyes on her. They were black, with a nasty glint of red. 'Has nobody told you?' he purred.

'Told us?'

'Was because you left lunch,' said Vlad. 'People wiz good manners hear things. Death Eric has New Look.'

'Wha,' said Lou and Buddy, together.

'Feedback Metal is so lasst lifetime,' said Vlad. 'Now is time for vider horizon. I am happy to announce that under new management Death Eric is playing Whirl Music –'

'*Wha?*' said Buddy and Lou. 'Whirl music? *Dad?*'

The spot settled on Eric. He stood up. He looked pained.

'Pies,' he said. 'Me belly hurts.'

Suddenly Wave was behind him, wearing her fur hat and her glittering Honganian smile.

'Announcement first, Eric darling,' she said. 'Then *and only then*, indigestion pills.'

'Oh,' said Eric. 'Yeah. Honganian Whirl Music. Cool. Gimme the pills.'

'Oi,' said Buddy, whose head was spinning with disbelief. 'What about the rest of the band?'

'They had a chance to vote,' said Vlad. 'But they seem to be avay. So they can like it or lump it.'

Eric stirred in his chair. 'Er . . .' he said.

'So that's all right, dollink,' said Wave, sitting on his knee and patting his face. 'Hongania Slobodna brodnye! Welcome to the New Look!'

'Slobodna brodnye!' cried the many people with big moustaches and fur hats among the columns. Someone started to twing an ood. Someone else made a cow noise on a skveezebox. Someone started to sing through a mouthful of pie. Suddenly the Hall of Columns was full of ghastly folk music.

Buddy and Lou watched, horrorstruck. A small

man in a fur hat folded his arms and started to dance. He leaped many feet into the air, collided with the ceiling and fell stunned. The music clattered on.

'Enid,' said Lou, 'let us get out of here.'

The children pushed the gigantic roadie into a small drawing room upholstered in purple velvet and shot the bolt on the door. 'What *is* this?' they said, together.

'What's what?' said Enid. She looked as if she knew something had gone wrong but had no idea what.

'Handing over control of Death Eric to this Vlad –'

'There was a vote,' said Enid. 'Your mum voted. Your dad voted. Nobody voted against them.'

'How about you?'

Enid gazed in an agonized manner at the tattooed skeletons dancing ring-a-ring o'roses on her vast knee. 'It's Vlad,' she said. 'He's so . . . well, *masterful*.' She came to a halt.

'Traitor,' said Buddy.

Lou stamped on his foot. 'Tell us,' she said, girl to woman.

Enid shrugged. 'You know what it is? Every time

I see someone come along and start making decisions, my heart turns to golden syrup.'

Lou rolled her eyes. Enid just could not be trusted around men with Authority.

'We'll take care of this,' said Buddy grimly. 'Because it says in the Band Rules music policy votes belong to the Manager, Wave, Dad and the Rhythm Section, i.e. Fingers and Kenyatta.'

'So if Mum was gone,' said Lou. 'And the band was back together, and playing the old type stuff, and liking it enough to vote for it, that would be three votes i.e. the band to one i.e. the manager with one person abstaining i.e. not voting i.e. Mum.'

'Ye-es,' said Enid, looking slightly dazed. 'But the record company wants a New Look –'

'Never mind New Looks,' said Lou. 'You just watch out for that Vlad. He's no good.'

'Yeah.' Enid brightened. 'Well, I'll get them recording. Maybe when Eric actually hears this Whirl Music he'll kick them out.' She stumped out of the drawing room, much braced by her plan.

'Poor Enid,' said Lou.

'Woo,' said a voice.

Buddy glanced round, saw a tall figure of vaguely rock-and-roll aspect leaning against a wall, and said, 'Go away.'

'Woo,' said the voice.

'Perhaps you are not with me,' said Buddy. 'Off you go. We are in a meeting.'

'WAAAGH,' said the figure. It was wearing a cloak.

'Go *away*,' said Buddy.

'WOOO,' said the figure, much more loudly this time. It wrapped itself huffily in its cloak and disappeared. There was a clap of thunder and a flash of lightning. Lumps of plaster fell out of the ceiling.

'Ask yourself, was that necessary?' said Buddy.

'Buddy,' said Lou in a thin voice, 'that door is closed.'

'Course it is,' said Buddy.

'I mean, it was never open. But that person went out through it.'

'Wha.'

'I mean, that person came into the room through a closed door and left the same way. Don't you *understand*?' said Lou. 'That must have been the *Ghost*!'

'Oh. It looked . . . well, I thought it would be kind of spookier than that.'

'I thought it was a bit spooky,' said Lou.

'Like I said, what's dead can't hurt you,' said Buddy, yawning. 'Plus, where were we brought up?'

'In the roaring heart of rock and roll,' said Lou.

'Which can be *really* scary. And you're still frightened of ghosts?'

Lou shook her head admiringly. 'Right as usual, dear brother. Now. We have a problem. What do we do with problems?'

'We solve 'em,' said Buddy, whose mouth was perhaps a little drier than usual. You could act casual about ghosts, but that did not necessarily mean you *felt* casual about them.

But Lou's mind was on the problems of the new album. 'Now then,' she said. 'Ghosts aside. First, we introduce the Turkey to the Swallow.'

'Wha?'

'Mum to Libby.'

'Oh. Yeah. But what about the New Look?'

'Never mind that. First, we've got a band to get together.'

'How?'

'They may not be answering their phones, but we know where they are. So we'll get Enid to take us travelling. To pay some visits.'

'Heh, heh,' said Buddy.

'Heh, as you say, heh,' said Lou.

3

'Doom, doom, doom,' hummed Fingers Trubshaw to himself. His thumbs were hooked into the armholes of his tweed waistcoat, his brown shoes twinkled in the sun, and a warm breeze fluttered the ribbons of the rosette on his lapel. On the rosette were printed in gold letters the words CHIEF STEWARD. Around him milled crowds of people with clean straw hats and dirty fingernails. It was the Hell Sea Flower Show, and Fingers Trubshaw was on his stand, a handkerchief-sized lawn of the purest green –

Hang on.

About now you will be saying, this is the world of Feedback Metal and we have just met a ghost and flower shows are not even one tiny bit rock and roll, so who is this Trubshaw and what is all this boring gardening doing in the story?

Perfectly reasonable question.

Fingers Trubshaw is a geezer with a medium-sized stomach, quite a lot of curly brown hair, and a squashy red nose. According to Death Eric fans, Fingers Trubshaw's main job in life is to be the bass guitarist of Death Eric. But according to Fingers Trubshaw his main job in life is to be the Managing Director of Green Fingers Trubshaw, the country's foremost lawncare company. He quite likes playing bass guitar. But the thing that gives him maximum satisfaction is to allow his eyes to rest upon a stretch of velvety green turf.

Which was what he was doing at the flower show.

For years, Fingers Trubshaw had been after the job of CHIEF STEWARD (Lawns). The last CHIEF STEWARD (Lawns) had retired two weeks ago at the age of ninety-six, his harpoon having been struck by lightning after he had been stalking a mole for three days and nights. And Fingers had been appointed in his stead. Fingers smiled, wagging his head. Soon, His Maj would be poling up to shake hands and ask him what he did. And Fingers would be able to say, 'Lawncare.' His Maj was known to be very, very keen on lawns. Fingers would score many points.

Fingers Trubshaw straightened his pink tweed tie. The crowd had fallen silent. Policemen were making the way clear for a tall man in a blue suit and a summer-weight crown. The tall man was smiling and talking to a rose bush. The rose bush bowed slightly, though it might have been the wind. His Maj passed on. And was now heading straight for the Green Fingers Trubshaw stand. Fingers passionately desired his Award of Lawn Merit (Gold Star). It would be a dream come true. It would make him the greatest lawn expert on the planet.

Fingers cast a glance out of the corner of his eye at the stand. The lawn was immaculate . . .

Except for the large bear sitting in the middle of it with its tongue hanging out.

'Oi,' said a voice. 'The band needs you.'

Fingers knew without looking that the owner of the voice was Buddy Thrashmettle. His heartbeat sped up a bit.

'Go away,' he said. 'I'm busy.'

'So will that bear be any minute now,' said Buddy. 'He's a Digging Bear. On the word of command, he digs.'

Fingers felt the blood drain from his head. 'Noo,' he said.

'Come back then. Right now. Immediately. We need you at Castle Bones to vote on a most important matter.'

'Won't,' said Fingers.

'Don't say you weren't warned,' said Buddy.

'Go away,' hissed Fingers.

His Maj seemed to have got into an argument with a dahlia. Fingers' hand closed round a square plastic object in his pocket, and squeezed.

'I'm counting to three,' said Buddy. 'Then I do the special whistle and the bear is like, where's Australia?'

'Count, then,' said Fingers.

Looking up at the bass player over the slopes of the tweed waistcoat, Buddy thought he was looking . . . well, rather *smug*. Ooer, he thought. 'One,' he said.

There was a slight stirring in the crowd.

'Two,' he said.

The slight stirring became a commotion. Two men in blue uniforms popped out of the mass of people.

'You paged, sir?' they said to Fingers.

'Remove this child,' said Fingers. 'And that bear.'

'Dig, Bruin!' cried Buddy. But one of the blue uniforms was already leading the bear away. And the other blue uniform was leading Buddy away.

As Buddy went, he saw the tall man in the suit and crown stop opposite Fingers. He heard the tall man say, 'And what do *you* do?'

He heard Fingers say, 'Once, I was a bass guitarist. But now I do lawncare.'

'*Much* better,' said His Maj.

Not so, thought Buddy.

Already he was scheming Phase 2, No More Mr Nice Guy.

Kenyatta McClatter was wearing white today. His shoes were white, and so were his trousers and his tunic and his wipe-clean vinyl tam-o'-shanter with small albino sea urchin instead of pom-pom. All in all, he looked like what he was, i.e. a Scot of Kenyan extraction, prepared for a busy day's fish frying in the demonstration kitchen at Alfie

Tank's Academy of Sizzle. It was going to be a great day, and Kenyatta had been looking forward to it for ages. They were going to be doing Advanced Cod –

Hang on. What, you will be saying, is this all about? One moment it was all Feedback Metal and Band Votes, with a strong element of Ghosts. Then we went to the flower show. And now we are at a cookery school in Dem. Too confusing. Why should we bother?

Good point. Explanation follows.

If you had asked Kenyatta McClatter what he did in life, he would have told you that he fried fish. After a few minute's conversation about coley, salmon, Mars bars and African fry pies, you might have noticed that Kenyatta's hands were seldom still, moving around the neighbouring pots, pans and human heads with a reebap, a reebap, a rittli-bipplireebap sort of rhythm. And if he got round to explaining, he might have mentioned that on the very few occasions he was not frying fish he was playing drums for Death Eric. Actually he quite liked playing drums for Death Eric, as a sort of hobby. But his main ambition was to rise to the top of the fish-frying tree. Which was why he was here at the Academy of Sizzle, as seen on TV, the country's foremost fish-frying school.

The bit of hagfish in the fryer was bubbling nicely. Further down the row of Advanced Fryers, a very fat man in a grease-stained apron and a tall chef's hat was swearing horribly at something that had once been an octopus. This was Alfie Tank. It was important to make a good impression on Alfie Tank if you were going to get your Class A Certificate. Kenyatta passionately wanted the Class A Certificate. The final test lay a few days in the future, as long as all went well today and Alife approved the hagfish. The hagfish was an important stepping stone.

'Psst,' said a voice beside him.

Kenyatta's eyes swivelled sideways. He saw a small girl with a Venetian red blazer, a neatly pressed box-pleat skirt, and an expression of deep concentration.

'Lou!' he said. 'Howzit? Look, can this wait? I'm busy.'

'No,' said Lou, firmly. 'We want you to come to Castle Bones right now immediately and vote on a most important band matter.'

'Sorry,' said Kenyatta, giving her an enormous

white smile slightly tinged with anxiety. 'I got me hagfish en croute to think about –'

'Oh, dear,' said Lou. Her hand came out of her pocket holding something. 'Then I am going to have to throw this blue dye in your fryer and, as everyone knows, it is impossible to eat blue food, so you will have to –'

'CARAMBA!' roared the voice of Alfie Tank, as heard on TV. 'WOZZIS? SOMEONE IN MY KITCHEN IS WEARIN' A COLOUR OTHER THAN WHITE? SHAME! OUT! *VOETSAK!* SCRAM!' Alife towered over her like a large white-and-purple thundercloud.

'But –' said Lou.

The air around the world-famous chef's head became blue and hazy. Lou had always lived in the rather rude world of Feedback Metal. Even so, several of the words Alife used were new to her.

'I merely –'

'DON'T YOU MERELY ME!' roared Tank. 'OUT! OUT! OUT!'

'This way, Miss,' said a large assistant chef with SECURITY written round the front of his hat.

'But –'

66

'Butter me no buts,' said the security chef, grasping her firmly by the dye-hurling arm.

Lou found herself marching towards the exit. Behind her, she could hear the maestro speaking of Kenyatta's hagfish.

'Exquisite!' he was crying. '☠ ✖ ☢⚠ fabulous! So ⚠✖🗲🔥 subtle!'

'Oo,' Kenyatta was saying. 'Glad you like it, er, Alfie.'

'CALL ME MAESTRO, INSECT!' bellowed the Great Fryer.

The door closed.

'Missing you already, little girl,' said the security chef.

Lou climbed into the limo.

'How did it go?' said Enid, who was driving.

'Oh, fine,' said Lou. She leaned back on the genuine lizardskin cushions and did not answer.

She was already plotting Phase 2, No More Ms Nice Girl.

The dark woods of Castle Bones stretched out and hugged the limos to their chilly bosom. A grim racket of skveezeboxes and oods filled the Hall of Columns. Lou and Buddy could not face going in, so they walked down to the lake. As they passed the rabbit hole, the buzzing noise seemed extra loud. Lou stooped and frowned.

'Two voices,' she said. Then her eyes opened wide. She looked at her brother. His eyes were open wide too. 'The Turkey and the Swallow have met!' she cried. 'Can it be working?'

'I'll check,' said Buddy.

'Don't rock the boat.'

'Obviously not.'

They walked down the steps and peered into the cave. The boulder with the smiley face was still there, obviously. Libby Squid was there too, floating a couple of centimetres off the ground. And so was the children's mother.

'No more Honganian hat,' said Lou breathlessly.

'And no leather boots,' said Buddy. 'The Turkey has Flown.'

Actually, Wave was wearing yellow pyjamas. Holy yogic *saffron* yellow. The children tiptoed away.

'Thank you, Brothers Grime,' breathed Lou, when they were outside again.

They walked over to the kitchen. Cookie was in there, looking harassed.

'How's it going?' said Buddy.

'Cauldron only turned to blood after lunch as per usual, dinnit.'

'Yuk. What's for supper?'

'Honganian pies.'

'Again?'

'If it isn't pies, it's "Where's me pies?" So it's pies,' said Cookie. 'Gets you down after a bit.'

'We'll cook 'em today,' said Lou.

'You? Cook?'

'If you tell us what's in them.'

'Flour. Lard. Suet. Potatoes. That's your heavy pie.'

'Ah,' said the children. 'Good. Why don't you go and watch some telly?'

'Can't wait,' said Cookie, unlashing his apron. 'Give you the creeps, this place does. Blood and pies.'

He stumped out of the kitchen, still muttering.

'All right,' said Lou. 'Let's get to work.'

'But you can't cook,' said Buddy.

'Obviously not,' said Lou. 'Now are you going to stand there talking all night, or are you going to pass the suet?'

Eric was sitting on a low stool. He was hunched over his legendary guitar Rabid Dingo, a night-black

Gibson Flying V battered and covered in tooth-marks, half-listening to Vlad, who was trying to teach him a Honganian whirl tune.

'Wha,' he said.

'It's easy,' said Vlad, flicking a cowlick of black hair out of his scornful eyes. 'First, Sergei plays whang clang bang infectious Honganian intro, sound of happy workers arriving in tractor factory. Then Boris comes in with fiddle, makes inspiring noise of workers working while bats fly in air above production line. Then Ivan plays mighty chord on skveeze-box to sound like hooter going for lunch break. Then you are comink in with Rabid Dingo solo to make eating of heavy pies happy sound.'

'Pthh,' said Eric from behind purple curtains of hair. 'Sounds 'orrible.'

'No, does not,' said Vlad. 'Then Igor start to dance and hey presto! Whirl music! New Look!'

'You said about a bat,' said Eric, who had obviously taken in none of the above, it being too long, too complicated and frankly not interesting enough.

Vlad bared his large sharp teeth in a rather worrying smile.

'Rrrr,' he said. 'So. A-vun, two – Where are you goink?'

For Eric had laid his guitar aside and was clambering to his feet.

'Dunno yet,' he said.

Vlad said, 'We must play music. Or Mrs Wave will be disappointed.'

The visible parts of Eric's face went pale.

'Ooer,' he said. 'Many bats, many.' He sat down again and picked up his guitar.

'Other way up,' said Vlad. 'Now. A-vun, a-two —'

'Yoo-hoo!' cried Buddy's voice from the shadows of the Hall of Columns. 'Lunchtime!'

'The pies are cooked!' cried Lou. 'They lie steaming on the great table, ready for all!'

'Hoopla!' cried Igor, folding his arms and springing wildly into the air.

'Pies!' cried one and all, casting aside their instruments and surging towards the dining room.

As they sat down, Wave came in. She was dressed in yellow pyjamas. The black hat and mad Honganian smile had gone. Instead her hair was cut very short and a scarlet bindi glowed between her eyebrows. Courteously, Buddy fetched her a chair. She muttered something about not needing earthly things, sat down cross-legged on the seat next to Libby Squid and began a conversation with her, raising her voice to be heard above the Honganians, who were tuning their own voices up for a merry song.

'Is an important song,' said Vlad. 'The people are hungry but now they can see pies coming. Is called title "Happily Waiting for Arrival of Pies". Words are Will they be heavy, will they be Thick and Contain so much Suet you'll want to be Sick.'

'How apt,' said Lou, noticing that her mother had stopped talking and turned a weird greenish hue. 'Pie, Mum? Enid, carve.'

Enid plunged a knife into the sweaty, whitish surface of the pie. A thick red liquid welled up round the blade. Even the Honganians fell silent, except for Vlad, who seemed to be panting a bit.

'Ooer,' said Sid the Soothsayer. 'That's . . .'

'Blood!' shrieked Wave, leaping on to her chair and making a sign against the Evil Eye. 'Unclean!'

'Rich red splendid lovely blood!' cried Buddy with cleverly faked enthusiasm. 'Hongania's favourite gravy! Come 'n' get it! If you can't slop it up with your knife and fork, spoons are available! Hey! Mum! Where are you going?'

Wave had made it as far as the door without

apparently touching the ground, closely followed by Libby Squid. 'Rishikesh! With LiBi Squiddartha! To the yoga ashram of Swami Barmi! Whole grains! Spring water! Levitation!'

'Will you send a postcard?' said Lou.

'Just so we can be sure you're safely there,' said Buddy.

'Yeah, ugh, unclean,' said Wave. She blew some hasty kisses. 'Mwah, mwah. Missing you already. Enid! The airport!'

'Aye, aye,' said Enid, pushing her plate away and avoiding Vlad's eye in case of Love Hypnosis. 'See you later, kids.' Pause. Hoarse whisper. 'Actually, I dunno if I fancy blood.'

'Ah,' said Lou. 'That was just our little joke. Taste it.'

Enid put out a large but elegant finger, dabbed gingerly at the red ooze, and licked it. Suddenly her face resembled a huge rugged landscape with a sunrise happening at its edge.

'Ketchup!' she whispered.

'Don't tell Mum.'

Roadie, mother and the newly named LiBi Squiddartha departed. Silence fell, broken only by the sound of jaws on pies, the dismal hooting of

Flatpick the budgie, and some unpleasant noises coming from Vlad, who seemed disappointed not to have got real blood.

Buddy caught Lou's eye. 'Kitchen,' he mouthed. Lou pushed her plate away.

They slipped away and walked down the long, clammy corridors towards the kitchen.

'I must say,' said Buddy, 'that Vlad is not an easy person to like.'

'How true,' said Lou. 'Perhaps now that Mum has gone he'll go too.'

'I doubt it. Not while he's got Enid in his power.'

'Yes . . .' Pause. 'Do you know, I think it would be a good idea to arrange his undoing.'

'It will happen,' said Buddy, pushing open the kitchen door. 'Ah, Cookie. What did you think of our pies?'

'Totally disgusting,' said Cookie. 'So I stopped watching telly and done you lasagna.'

'Nice,' said Buddy, and for a longish time there were only eating noises, and grunts as Cookie pointed out particularly good bits of pepperoni and hard-boiled egg. Finally, everyone emitted small sighs of satisfaction, and Buddy said, 'So the cauldron turned to blood again.'

'Regular as clockwork, every day,' said Cookie.

'Did you save any?'

'Course,' said Cookie, reaching for a rack of test tubes on one of the new stainless-steel shelves. 'Total range of samples. Look.'

Lou and Buddy looked. 'Funny-looking blood,' said Buddy.

'Wha?'

'Look at it against the light. I mean, day one, that's blood all right. But day two, well, it looks all watery. Taste some.'

'Eur!' cried Lou.

'Less of that,' said Cookie, who had stuffed in an educated finger and licked it. ' 's Ribena.'

'*What?*'

'And the day after that is – (slurp) – passion-fruit squash. Then there's beetroot juice from concentrate. Then there's – dearie me, it's not even red – Blood Orange Crush followed by Orange Squash followed by Lemon Barley Water, which is hardly even *pretending* to be blood. I mean it's sort of greenish white. Cor stone me,' said Cookie, 'I wondered where all me squashes and cordials were going.' He frowned, scratching his small, bristly head. 'But I was in here at two today when the water in the cauldron turned to . . . looks like raspberry juice. And the cauldron lives on the fire, it's cemented in, like. So how did it *get* there?'

Buddy wiped his mouth with a fine linen napkin and stood up.

'If you will excuse me,' he said, 'I am going to take a look up the chimney.'

'Wha.'

But Buddy was already climbing the wrecked brickwork on the back of the soot-stained hearth.

'Ah,' he said. 'Steps, for when they used children as chimney sweeps. Agh.' His voice became muffled. 'Nothing. Wait. I have detected a spill. I am tasting it. I am getting . . . Ugh. Disgusting. All sooty.'

'What's all sooty?' said Lou. It was all very well for Buddy. He was a boy, and besides, he always wore black, so the soot would not show. There was no *way* you would get soot out of Venetian red.

'Ribena. Orange squash. I've found where it's coming from.'

'Where?'

'Fireplace,' said Buddy. 'Mmph. Argh. Up here somewhere. I'm going in.' More silence. A scuttering sound, and soot falling into the fireplace. Then Buddy's voice, very faint now. 'Room,' he said. 'Dust everywhere. No footprints. There's a . . . door. Locked.' Pause. Then his voice again, puzzled. 'From the inside. There's a key. I'll be with you in five.'

Five minutes later Buddy came through the kitchen door, hauling cobwebs out of his hair and decidedly out of breath.

'Someone,' he said, 'is going into that room and pouring Ribena and stuff down the chimney to try to make it look supernatural.'

'Someone who doesn't leave footprints,' said Lou.

'Yes.'

'And who can get into a room with a door locked –'

'A big door, with a very heavy lock –'

'– from the inside. So whoever it is probably *is* supernatural.'

Brother and sister stared at each other, wide-eyed.

'*Cool!*' they said.

A day passed. The Honganians played. Enid came back from the airport full of fight, and was reduced to jelly by Vlad's dreadful eyes. Lou and Buddy made a plan. At one fifty-five next day, they were ready to carry it out.

*

It was an ordinary Castle Bones room, sorry, chamber. There was panelling, black oak, head-high. Above the panelling someone had painted a Dance of Death, with peasants skipping and demons shoving them into a burning fiery furnace. In the middle of the wall was a window, heavily barred. What light could get through the bars then crawled through some cobwebs, tripped over a mouse's nest and fell into the shadows between some large, lumpy and none-too-clean pieces of furniture grouped round a fireplace of massy stone. A chance ray stumbled over an eyeball. It was a modern eyeball, veined and rolling. It was situated in the head of BB, a junior roadie. Also in the room, sorry, chamber, were Big Enid hiding behind a large settle, Rick the Thick hiding unsuccessfully behind rather a small book, Buddy and Lou hiding successfully behind chairs, and Sid the Soothsayer, not hiding at all, but complaining.

'I dunno why we are waitin' here,' he said. 'Ghosts don't exist and even if they do it'll never come.'

'It has to,' said Buddy. 'Two p.m. daily, cauldron turns to blood. Always happens.'

'Never,' said Sid sulkily.

There was silence while everyone reflected that Sid was such a hopeless soothsayer that you could be sure that the opposite of what he said would happen would happen. Then there was not silence any more.

'Wozzat noise?' said Rick the Thick.

'Teeth,' said Buddy.

'Sid's teeth,' said Lou. 'Chattering.'

'I think I may have really seen the actual future,' said Sid, in a voice that shook. 'Any minute now –'

'Ssh!' said Buddy. He tightened his grip on a string of garlic. Lou shifted her hands on the handle of a bucket of holy water. Various roadies and soothsayers crept behind crucifixes, amulets, and in Rick the Thick's case a sirloin steak he had nicked from the fridge and been trying to sharpen, though he could not for the life of him see how he could drive it through anything's heart –

'Here it comes!' hissed Lou.

Buddy looked at the back of his hand. The hairs were standing straight up. The air in the room had become suddenly cold. From where he crouched, he could see a whitish vapour creeping under the door. The vapour piled up into a mound and began to thicken. Rick the Thick was holding his steak in one hand and his book in the other. His mouth fell open. So did his hands. He rushed to the door and shook it. It stayed shut. He rushed to the fireplace and scrambled up the chimney and out of sight. There was a scrabbling, a cry, a splash, and the sound of someone swearing horribly.

Fallen down the chimney, into the Great Cauldron, and Cookie raising objections, guessed Buddy –

'WHA?' said a deep and awful voice, like skulls rolling in an empty coffin.

Buddy realized he did not want to look at whoever it was that owned this voice. He put out his hand sideways. Lou took it. Her fingers felt very cold.

'SOMEONE IS HERE,' said the deep and awful voice. Not skulls in an empty coffin. Gravel on the lid of a *full* coffin –

'Oi,' said Enid, standing up. 'Did you know you was trespassing? Wot you look like I will not say, except that you are way way too bony and that cloak –'

'Shroud.'

'– shroud, then, is in a shocking state, needs a good wash –'

'Who threw that?' said the voice which, now Buddy came to look, belonged to a two-metre-tall skeleton with straggly red hair and a mouldy green cloak, sorry, shroud. 'Garlic's hard, you know. Who?'

Naturally, nobody answered. The Ghost got huffy. It stamped a foot. 'Garlic doesn't *work* on ghosts,' it said. 'That's vampires. Ignorance!' It threw back its ghastly head and uttered a peal of blood-freezing laughter.

Buddy and Lou were not watching its head.

They were looking at its boots.

Its lizardskin cowboy boots. With the lizards' heads on the toes.

'I think I'm going to faint,' said Sid the Soothsayer. Remarkably, he crashed to the floor, raising a crowd of dust.

'Nice boots, Ghost,' said Buddy.

'Oo,' said the Ghost. 'Ta,' it simpered. Not a pretty sight.

Lou had been frowning. The hair, the boots . . . 'Haven't I seen you somewhere before?' she said. 'Besides that once.'

The Ghost tossed its head. One of its eyeballs fell out, rolled across the floor, scampered back to its owner and shot up its shroud.

'Very probably,' it said.

'You used to be really *famous*!' said Lou.

'*Used to be?*' said the Ghost. 'I'll have you know that my records still sell easy as many – what's that?

Far away in the house, something had said BONG.

'The Tower clock,' said Buddy. 'Striking –'

'*Two!*' shrieked the Ghost. 'Oo, I've absolutely *got* to, it is *ordained* that I – that is, lo the Great Cauldron turns to blood on the stroke of two daily!'

Rushing to the fireplace it leaned into the chimney and emptied a bag of something into the darkness. Far below, there was a fizzing sound, closely followed by the sound of Cookie swearing again.

'Blood?' said Buddy. 'I don't think so.'

'Obviously it's blood,' said the Ghost, emerging from the fireplace brushing soot off its shroud with a bony hand.

'No,' said Lou. 'I can smell it from here. It is my own Pink Rose Fizzy Bath Salts and I think you are a creep to swipe them.'

The Ghost looked at her, which was not all that pleasant, because its missing eyeball was now climbing up its face. The eyeball found its socket, settled in and focused on Lou.

'Well, sorry I'm sure,' said the Ghost sniffily. 'And now I suppose you are going to magic me into a bottle and bung me up with melted lead and put me under running water so I can no longer trouble your smelly little existence.'

'Wha?' said Lou and Buddy, mystified.

'Well, no dice,' said the Ghost. 'Insects!' it boomed, and now its voice seemed to fill the whole room. 'Repent and beware!'

At this point Enid, who did not approve of this kind of behaviour towards anyone called Thrashmettle, picked up the poker and walloped the Ghost as hard as she could. Obviously the poker went straight through. A frightful yell of laughter tore the air. Thunder boomed and plaster fell from the ceiling. The Ghost flung the shroud round its face. The tall figure became short and fat, then sank into a pile of something absolutely disgusting which steamed, shrank and vanished.

'Good riddance!' said Lou, who had actually turned rather pale.

'Quite so,' said Buddy, frowning.

'You OK?' said Enid.

'Of course we are,' said Lou. 'This Ghost is just attention seeking. We should ignore it and concentrate on the main thing, which is to get the band back together and make the new album and live happily ever after.'

'And send the Honganians away,' said Enid.

'Even Vlad?' said Lou.

'I love him,' said Enid. 'But I know he's a wrong 'un.'

'Don't worry,' said Lou. 'The main thing is, we love you. Don't we, Buddy?' She gently nudged her brother.

'Hmm,' said Buddy, looking slightly as if his mind was elsewhere.

'Buddy!' said Lou.

'History,' said Buddy. 'Research.'

'BUDDY!' roared Lou.

'Ahem,' said Enid. 'I think you will find that your brother is thinking.'

'This is no time for *thinking*!' said Lou. 'This is a time for –'

'Come downstairs,' said Buddy. 'There's something we should be looking at.'

'Wha.'

'In the Library. Something that will help with the Honganians.'

*

It was an enormous room. Three of the walls were lined with mouldering books, trophies of smashed electric guitars, and drum kits which had been kicked to bits by drummers. The fourth wall consisted of a huge stained-glass window, which at this time of day cast pools of light, red and green and gold, on the rich carpet and the leather-topped table that ran down the middle of the room.

'The window,' said Buddy.

'So?' said Lou.

Her brother was pointing, a dark, lanky form silhouetted against the light.

In the central panel was a picture of a man with an explosion of red hair. In the man's hand was a gold disc. Round the inside of the gold disc something was written: at least it looked like writing, but when Lou focused her eyes on it, it did not seem to mean anything.

'Wha?' she said.

'The hair. The boots,' said Buddy.

Lou peered at the boots. 'Goodness.' The hair was brilliant red. Like the hair of the Ghost. The boots were made of lizardskin. Like the boots of the Ghost. 'It's him,' she said.

Buddy was not listening. He was scuttling around

the library with a wheelbarrow made of pure mahogany, plucking out a book here, a book there. He wheeled the whole lot over to the table, licked his thumb and started leafing through pages.

Finally he said, 'There. Look.'

Lou looked.

The book was a copy of *The Rock and Roll Hall of Fame*. It was about fifty years old. The headline said GREATEST EVER STUFF. A smaller headline said *What is Metal and Will It Catch On?* Next to the big print was quite a lot of small print, which Lou did not bother to read, because she was looking at the picture.

The picture was of three men with long hair and embarrassing clothes made of satin and sheepskin. One of them had eyebrows that grew into his hair, so he was probably a drummer. The other looked like a starved ape, so he was probably a bass player. The third was very tall and very thin. His hair was a bright, weird red, and stuck out from his head like the business end of a lavatory brush. His boots were cowboy boots made of lizardskin, with the lizards' heads actually on the toes. ALUMINIUM DAVE, said the caption. MAN OR MONSTER?

'Do you mean,' said Lou, 'that that horrible-looking thing in those very cool boots that pinched my bath salts was the ghost of Aluminium Dave Krang?'

Her brother raised his chin in a rather irritating way and opened another book.

'Press clippings,' he said. 'All about Aluminium Dave. They start with him buying the place, ancient Castle Bones, evil reputation, bla, bla.' He turned a page. 'Here we are. Two years later. "Star Aluminium Dave Krang, the man seen by many as the pioneer of heavy metal, has vanished at his recording-studio castle. Last person to see him was Colin Ancient, his personal road manager. 'The Big Transformer was overheating,' said Ancient, 23. 'It was blocked cooling-water ducts. We was mixing the new album so time was running out. Dave was a keen diver so he went down to see if he could clear them. He never came back. It is well heavy. Obviously we will never release the album, the pain would be too awful. Did I say it is well heavy? Because it is. Heavy, I mean.'"'

'So he drowned in the lake,' said Lou. 'How dreadful.'

'Wait,' said Buddy, doing a bit more leafing. 'Here's another. *Marie Antoinette* magazine. It's an article about rockers who have turned into peasants.

Look. Not there. Here.' Buddy put his finger on a photograph. It showed a thin man leaning against one side of a pointed doorway, just about to throw quite a big turnip at the photographer. The thin man was bald, and bent just about double. 'It says here, "Colin Ancient, once personal roadie to Metal star Aluminium Dave Krang, still lives in the gate lodge of Castle Bones, scene of the tragedy that wrecked his life." It's him.'

'Certainly is,' said Lou. 'So the Ghost is the ghost of Dave Krang and our gatekeeper knows more than he's letting on.'

'Yup,' said Buddy.

'But how can we get him to talk?'

'Blackmail,' said Buddy.

'Obviously. I was just thinking aloud,' said Lou. 'Shall we go?'

'We'll take Enid.'

'Better still,' said Buddy, 'Enid will take us.'

4

As the limo rolled up to the gate, the old bald bent person came out of the little Gothic lodge. Even through the windows Buddy and Lou could hear the clonk as his knees hit his chin.

'It's him all right,' said Lou, getting out.

The gatekeeper knuckled what had once been a forelock with a bony forefinger.

'Ello young master and missy,' he said, casting a cunning glance at the dim shape of Enid, half-visible behind the smoked-glass driver's window. 'What an honour arr to be sure –'

'Highly convincing,' said Buddy.

'But we know who you are,' said Lou. 'And we want to ask you some questions.'

Colin Ancient stopped being a prehistoric rustic and began to look like an elderly roadie.

'Yeah?' he said.

'About the ghost of Aluminium Dave Krang.'

'Who?' said Colin Ancient.

The limo window rolled down a bit.

'Mornin', Colin,' said Enid, with a lovely smile that showed her many teeth and granite jaw. 'Everything OK, children?'

'Will be soon,' said Lou, with an extra-sweet smile of her own. 'When Colin has decided he does not want to be evicted and answers our questions.'

'OK, OK,' said Colin. 'What's the question?'

'The Ghost,' said Buddy. 'We think he could be very very useful to us.'

'We just want to get to know him better,' said Lou.

Colin's eyes narrowed. 'Good luck,' he said. 'One of the first things he done when he started haunting was put Spangles McFee in a loony bin, did you know that?'

'Eek,' said Buddy and Lou, rightly horrified.

'But why did he turn into a ghost?' said Buddy.

'Well, we were making an album, and things started to go weird. I mean it is not normal to break all the strings on your guitar at once five songs running. Then the drummer fell into his tom-tom and did not bounce off the skin because it wasn't a skin at all, the drum was full of milk. And things kept happening, so people said it was the Castle Bones Curse. But we sort of soldiered on and kept the Curse at bay until we were doing the last big mix. It was late, and it was raining. And we were just getting to the last track, when this thunderstorm kicks in. And Dave shouts something like, "Oi, Curse, go and find someone else to bother!" joking, like. Then there was a big flash of lightning and a boom and the lights went out and the library window blew in and the Big Transformer fuses exploded and so Dave put on his diving gear and went into the lake to mend it and . . . ooer'

'Wha?'

'He never came back. And I was chopping wood a week later when I seen something.'

'What?' said Lou.

'Sort of a phantom,' said Ancient. 'Very tall. A sort of skellington, or at least a bit nibbled-looking. It was Dave. He wanted his boots.'

'Boots?' said Buddy.

'Them with the lizards on. He said even ghosts had feet and he asked me to leave them in the library on the table. Then he vanished, poof. So I found the boots and put them where he had said. Next day I went into the library and the boots were gone. And there on the table was a bit of paper written on in a wobbly hand, with instructions for a new window design. So we built the window and put it in. Then Gothalinda bought the castle and let me stay. Now I spose I get evicted.'

Buddy scowled. This had been less helpful than he had hoped. He said, 'But you have no way of getting in touch with the Ghost?'

'No,' said Ancient. 'It's not, we get in touch with him, it's more, he scares the living daylights out of us.'

'But ghosts usually want something,' said Lou, who was a great reader. 'Eternal peace. Something like that.'

'Dave? Peace? Don't make me laugh,' said the old roadie. 'I've seen some show-offs in my time.

But the biggest show-off of the lot was Aluminium Dave. Eternal peace, hah! Infernal noise more like.'

'Ah,' said Lou.

'Interesting,' said Buddy.

'So, am I evicted?' said Ancient.

The window rolled down. 'So far so good,' said Enid. 'But watch your step. Get in, kids.'

Lou sank back in the luxurious seat and glanced sideways at her brother. The finely chiselled features were still and pale under the spiky black hair. She could tell he had an idea. There was no sense hurrying him, though. So she looked out of the window and counted birds of ill omen, including crows, ravens, magpies, cassowaries and owls barn, little, screech and eagle. There were thirteen in all between the gate and the castle.

As the limo drew to a halt, Buddy said, 'I think the Ghost might like to get out and about a bit.'

A normal sister would have stared at her brother making eyes-crossed faces with added forehead tapping and duh noises. Not Lou. Buddy was one of the most brilliant people she had ever met, except of course her. He would tell her his idea in time, and you could be sure it would be worth waiting for.

Unlike the sound that walloped her ear when Enid opened the limo door.

The children climbed on to the carpet of bones in front of the castle. The front door was open. From the darkness within came the awful sound of ood music. Over it, high and dirty as a pair of cowman's boots, soared the angelic tones of Eric Thrashmettle's guitar.

'Cor, he can play!' breathed Enid. 'Who needs a New Look?' Then she thought of Vlad, and went pink. Things would work out in the end, probably. Well, maybe. Well, just possibly . . . Her mind vanished in a pink fog. She rushed inside to see her beloved Inhaler.

'Yuk,' said Buddy.

Discreetly covering their ears against the oods and skveezeboxes, the Thrashmettle children passed through the Hall of Columns, along the Long Long Gallery and into the library.

'Right,' said Buddy. 'We need to make this ghost an offer he can't refuse. He can really help us out if we get him on side. But first, we need to summon him.'

'Well, there must be something in this library about ghosts,' said Lou.

They searched, then Buddy plunked a large book on the table. 'OK,' he said. 'So here we go.'

It was a long read and a boring one, the writing being weird.

'Take nine toads and a scale of ye Gryphon,' said Lou. 'You got nine toads?'

'Yuk, no way.'

'Ye Gryphon?'

'Gryphons are mythical.'

For the next four hours, the Thrashmettle children pored over recipes that got more and more disgusting. They considered candles made of bats, cats and reptile fats. Being children of high intellect and good sense, they rejected them all.

A roadie brought them ground Aberdeen Angus hamburgers on sesame-seed buns, topped off with sheep's milkshakes and followed by a nourishing salad. They ate, trying not to think about the disgusting stuff they had just read about. As they ate, they pondered.

'We need to get inside its mind,' said Lou at last.

'Ghosts don't have minds,' said Buddy.

'This one does,' said Lou. 'It likes its boots. This is a rock and roll ghost. A ghost with vanity, that likes to show off.'

'So?'

'This will be a ghost that will want to put things right. Like the Cooker of Cakes.'

'Wha.'

'You know, in the Brothers Grime. The Cooker of Cakes or Cake-cooker.' Lou's hand crept to the special pocket where she kept her *Tales from the Brothers Grime*. 'Read it.'

'Tell me,' said Buddy, who had had enough rummaging around in leather-bound volumes for one day.

'Right,' said Lou, needing (as always) no prompting when it came to the Brothers Grime. 'Once upon a time there was a Cooker of Cakes or Cake-cooker who cooked cakes for a rabble. One day, he got fed up with the rabble and said he would cook no more. So the Cake-cooker sat in a comfortable chair and watched the rabble try to cook its own cake by committee.

'Being a rabble, they had no idea. So they decided to make an angel cake, and everyone suggested an ingredient. Eggs, butter, sugar, flour, they said, while the Cake-cooker looked on smiling. Cinnamon, vanilla, they said. Salt and pepper (at which the Cake-cooker looked pained, but said nothing).

'At last, the biggest idiot in the whole rabble got up and said, "I like spinach. Put in spinach." And they prepared to add spinach to the cake mix.

'At which point the Cake-cooker discovered that he could not sit and watch while they wrecked a perfectly good angel cake with spinach. So he got up out of his chair and cried, "Hey! Let me!"

'So the rabble did. And the cake was delicious.'

'So?' said Buddy.

Lou rolled her eyes. For a scientific genius, her brother could be a total moron sometimes. She looked around. There had to be a harpsichord in here somewhere; it was that kind of room. Sure enough, there was one in the corner. She sat down at it, coughing slightly as the cloud of dust rose. She opened the lid and began to spread her fingers over the blackened ivories, picking out a tune.

'What's that?' said Buddy.

'"Bad Skoool",' said Lou. 'Ten weeks at number one for Aluminium Dave.'

She put her shoulders into it, whamming out the well-known riff. But with a wrong chord in it.

'Bad skoool,' she sang.

'Rotten teacher. Chalky git –'

'Hey,' said a voice. 'Wrong chord.'

'Is, too, Buddy,' said Lou, not looking round, whamming away at the keyboard. Then she noticed that the air had got cold and the little hairs on her arms were standing on end. 'But that's not Buddy, is it?' she said.

'N-no,' said Buddy's voice.

'It is I,' said a voice like the roar of crematorium flames. 'From the top. Verse one. Again, two three *four* –'

'I'll go away and learn it,' said Lou, rather frightened, but a bit triumphant too, because she had indeed played a wrong chord totally on purpose, so the Brothers Grime had been right again.

'And while you're here,' said Buddy, 'there is something we'd like to ask you.'

'I DO THE ASKING,' said the Ghost.

'Not this time,' said Buddy. 'Do you feel you are getting big enough audiences nowadays?'

'Yes, well, obviously,' said the Ghost.

Lou got the distinct impression it was lying.

'We can help you,' said Lou. 'But you'll have to help us.'

'And what we want you to do will actually be fun,' said Buddy.

'Fun?' said the Ghost, suddenly sounding almost

human (though obviously with a strong supernatural accent).

'Yep,' said Buddy. 'Tell me, Ghost, is it possible for you to travel away from Castle Bones?'

'I may be transported in a snuffbox in which lies a grain of castle earth. Not,' said the Ghost, sounding depressed, 'that anyone would ever want to take me anywhere. I mean look at the state of me.'

'We would,' said Lou.

'You would?

'We think you're very very fabulous,' said Lou.

'Oo,' said the Ghost.

'And now Lou will tell you what to do,' said Buddy.

'It goes like this,' said Lou.

Doom doom doom, hummed Fingers Trubshaw. He was feeling smug again. He usually felt smug, now that he had got away from Death Eric and was devoting himself to lawncare full time. This morning, he had extra reasons. He was at the controls of a Mark VII Titanic Lawnshava, with three-metre cutting frontage, four-tonne roller, operator stereo and cab aircon. He had completed the first of what were to be forty-eight perfect stripes on the hallowed turf of the Dukes Cricket Ground. Up in the Members' Stand, he knew, the Head Groundsman of the World Cricket Wicket Association was watching. Watching admiringly. The Titanic Lawnshava was a whole new concept in lawncare, and the Mark VII was the best yet. Fingers Trubshaw was a mere blade of grass away from getting the lawncare contract for every cricket ground in –

The telephone on the dashboard rang. Fingers adjusted his hands-free headset. 'GFT,' he said. 'CEO on the QT.'

'Fingers?' said a voice.

'Who's that?' said Fingers, a cold thrill of horror shooting around under his tweed waistcoat.

'Buddy,' said the voice.

'And Lou,' said another voice. 'Look up to the right of the clock.'

Fingers looked. Up by the clock on the Members' Stand, two little figures looked back. They waved. Fingers said, in a hollow voice, 'Nice to see you.' Enid was standing behind them, huge and silent.

'Probably not,' said Buddy.

'We've got a suggestion for you,' said Lou.

'Oh no you –'

'It's time the band made a new album,' said Buddy. 'Come down to Castle Bones.'

'No,' said Fingers. His hands tightened on the leather-padded steering wheel and he gazed contentedly at the turf ahead, green, velvety, and as perfect as only two hundred years of mowing and rolling could make it. 'No *way*. I am happy here. And do not think you can get down here and wreck my lawn with bears or something. There is a ring of steel round Dukes. There are electric fences, man-traps and spring-guns. And even if you got on to the ground, elite groundsmen would Taser you and drag you – What did you say?'

'Sigh,' said Lou.

'As in, she sighed,' said Buddy. He had taken something from his blazer pocket – a little box? Perhaps. He had opened the lid, and was making a sprinkling movement with his fingers. 'Because bears are so *last time around*.'

'Don't you come near me,' said Fingers Trubshaw with a growing sense of doom.

'We won't,' said Buddy.

'Look,' said Lou. 'We're still up here.'

High on the stand, the little figures waved.

Then they watched.

'Go away,' said Fingers. Something seemed to be sticking into his ribs. 'I need to concentreeeeeeyyyaAAGH!'

What was sticking into his ribs was a ribcage. 'How do you drive this thing?' said a voice like a death-rattle with words. A skeleton was sitting in the driver's seat beside him. A face covered in rags of skin looked round at him, full of polite enquiry. One of the eyeballs fell out.

'HREEEEE!' shrieked Fingers, activating the EMERGENCY RELEASE button on the cockpit canopy and hurling himself out of his seat. He landed with a thump on the turf, rolled over and sat up. Oh, dear, he thought, using a brain that did not seem to be functioning quite right, made a dent in the turf. He sat and waited for the Dead Man's Handle to spring back to the OFF position, bringing the Lawnshava to a gentle halt.

But the Lawnshava did not halt. It accelerated.

Well, thought Fingers in a high, shrill voice, that is what happens to a Dead Man's Handle when you have a real Dead Man at the mower controls.

Then he fainted.

Which was probably just as well.

*

'Nice one, Ghost,' said Buddy, watching.

Lou opened her mouth, and shut it again. It was easy to see that the Ghost had a rock and roll past and a somewhat supernatural present. Even Enid looked impressed.

For a split second the mower rolled on. Then the engine screamed, flames shot out of the exhaust, and it stood on its rear rollers in a fearsome lawn-care wheelie. The front end hit the ground again with a crash. Then it was off, front blades spinning. At first it only cut grass. But the engine note rose higher, and the cuttings streaming over the cab turned from green to brown.

'Impressive machine,' said Buddy.

The mower was soon cab-deep in a trench it had dug itself, heading for the boundary, spewing earth. It turned right in a sweeping curve. Screams of anguish came from the Members' Stand.

'Noooooo!' cried a voice. 'Not –'

'The wicket?' said Buddy, as the trench hurtled through the stripe of ground that was cricket's holiest of holies. ' 'Fraid so.'

'Any minute now,' said Lou, 'that ghost is going to go –'

'Rrrrr!' shrieked the voices from the stand.

The Lawnshava was invisible. Suddenly the plume of earth stopped.

'– underground,' said Lou.

A long dip appeared in the Dukes turf, as if the roof of a tunnel was falling in. The dip vanished under the Members' Stand.

'Quick!' said Enid. 'I'm off! Gimme the snuffbox! See you at the limo!'

'Certainly,' said Lou. 'Buddy?'

Together, they walked down to where Fingers Trubshaw was standing with his hands in his hair and his feet on the green, green turf.

The very small patch of green, green turf remaining. All around him, the once billiard-table-like sward of Dukes looked as if it had been strip mined.

'Fingers,' said Buddy, 'it is time we got you out of here.'

'Out?' said Fingers like a man in a dream.

'Somewhere there are roadies to protect you,' said Lou. She pointed to a medium-sized crowd of groundsmen and cricket enthusiasts who were galloping towards them. Some carried cricket bats, others stumps. All were weeping tears of purest rage. 'Meanwhile, stay close to us.'

Tightly packed together, the trio edged towards the car park. The crowd stopped short, cursing and weeping. None of them would take the risk of hitting a child.

It would not have been cricket.

The staff by the barriers of Dukes tube station saw a huge, beautiful, muscular woman march into the station. They saw her hurdle the barriers like a flying rhino. They opened their mouths to tell her she was under arrest, caught her hard and flashing eye, and changed their minds. Enid marched down on to Platform 3, made a mental calculation, and stationed herself by a large poster of a lady with a big smile and a bare middle.

A strange vibration made itself felt in the platform slabs. Enid reached into her large but chic handbag and pulled out a porcelain snuffbox. The vibration grew stronger. Several rats burst out of the wall, leaped off the platform, and scuttled into the tunnel. Passengers waiting for a train found that the air had turned strangely cold.

There was a crash and a roar and the howl of an engine. The bare midriff of the lady on the poster bulged outwards. Bricks spewed on to the platform, followed by two whirling blades and the cockpit of a mower. And in the cockpit of the mower was . . .

Women screamed. Three people fainted. The Ghost stood up and stepped on to the platform, throwing his mouldy shroud over his raggy shoulder with a rakish flip.

'What are you advertising?' said a small man who blinked a lot.

'Death Eric,' said Enid.

'Do you mind?' said the Ghost. 'Aluminium Dave.'

'Aluminium Dave's dead,' said the man.

Enid whipped the top off the snuffbox. 'In,' she said.

'But –'

'In, I said.'

'Boo,' said the Ghost sulkily, then, 'Eee!' as he stretched like chewing gum and vanished into the tiny box. Enid reached into the mower and turned off the engine. Then she stepped over the small man, who had fainted, and strode out of the station.

The limo purred its way back towards Castle Bones. The loudest sounds were the ticking of the clock and Fingers Trubshaw sobbing.

'Music will make you better,' said Lou soothingly.
'One down,' said Buddy. 'One to go.'

Kenyatta McClatter was having a lovely day. Most of his days were lovely, now that things had gone quiet with Death Eric and he was devoting himself to full-time fish frying. He was standing in the kitchen of Chateau Tank, Alfie Tank's world-famous hotel on the cliffs of Dem. He was wearing his fryer's whites. His face shone in the heat of the stoves. On all sides pans banged and clattered, sauces roared and sizzled, and chefs howled and swore, none louder than the great Alfie Tank himself. Kenyatta stood at his deep-fat fryer, watching a lobster steak frying to golden perfection in a light beer batter, drumming to the great chorus of the kitchen. A-clang sizzle clatterbang clatterbang zee, went the kitchen. A-reebap, a-rittlibap, a rittlibong boom, went Kenyatta with his spatula and his slotted spoon.

At that moment, in the restaurant beyond the kitchen door, a very fat man walked in and sat down on two chairs. The head waiter sprinted into the kitchen, white as a sheet, and whispered something in the ear of Alfie Tank, who had been cursing a haddock.

Immediately, Alfie Tank climbed on to a food-preparation surface.

'Listen up!' he roared. 'The inspector is here! Tonight is the night he decides whether or not we get the Golden Meatball Award! So he gets a PERFECT DINNER and anyone who makes even the TEENY WEENIEST mistake gets FRIED ALIVE!'

A silence fell. When Alfie Tank said something like that, he meant it.

'So, get your FRESH LOCAL INGREDI-ENTS,' roared Tank. 'And COOK THEM TO BITS! GO! SHOW NO MERCY!'

The noise started up again, all cooks, sous-chefs, commis chefs, chefs de batterie and washers-up thinking ooer as they worked. The only person not thinking ooer was Kenyatta, who was rittlibapping away with his implements, dreaming happily of the Class A Certificate that would be his after he had finished work tonight. All the other Advanced Fish Fryers had dropped out when the pressure had got too much for them. But Kenyatta had trained in Feedback Metal and Chip Vans. He could take any amount of pressure –

'Ahem,' said a smallish voice down by his fryer.

Kenyatta ceased his paradiddles and looked down. Two smallish faces looked back up at him.

'Lou!' he said, rather nervously. 'Buddy! Who let you in?'

'We just arrived,' said Lou.

'Via the dustbins,' said Buddy.

'Because we want to talk to you,' said Lou.

'The band,' said Buddy, 'is in mortal danger.'

'We need your vote,' said Lou. 'Mum brought back lots of Honganians and they are playing lousy Whirl Music and there is a manager called Vlad who is a creep, and the good name of the band is —'

'Whoah!' cried Kenyatta. 'With respect, I don' care about the band. The band is part of a past that I did not . . . what you doin' with that lickle box type thing?'

For Buddy had taken from his pocket a small but beautiful porcelain snuffbox. He held it over the fish fryer and opened the lid. A little puff of what might have been dust drifted into the harsh lights of the kitchen.

'YARRR!' bellowed a mighty voice.

'Children, that Mister Tank,' said Kenyatta, in a voice suddenly tense. The fryer was sizzling behind him, louder than before. Kenyatta started to sweat. His Class A Certificate was at stake and the Golden Meatball inspector was in. 'You got to get out.'

The noise of the fryer had become practically deafening. The kitchen floor shook to the thump of Chef Tank's enormous footsteps.

Something was happening in the oil.

Tank came to a halt alongside him. The oil was rising and bulging, and emitting green fumes that smelt absolutely ghastly. Kenyatta pasted a false grin on his face.

'And *WHAT*,' roared Tank with a face like mauve suet, 'DO YOU CALL *THIS*? VISITORS IN MY AREEEGH.'

Probably Tank had meant to say 'kitchen'. We shall never know. Because he had reeled back from the fryer with his hands over his eyes. The reason for this being that something was rising from the boiling oil. Something that was definitely not a lobster steak fried to golden perfection. Unless a lobster steak has a skull, skeletal ribs and the rest of a human skeleton, all neatly coated in batter and sizzling horribly.

Not a lobster steak, then. The ghost, actually, of Aluminium Dave Krang.

'Oo,' said Aluminium Dave in an awful piping voice. 'Hot, hot, *hot*!' He picked up a saucepan and fanned himself with it. Then he hopped out of the fryer and stalked across the floor, dripping oil. He shoved open the swing door into the dining room with a bony hand. 'Hooray!' he said, in a voice like the unblocking of a deep drain. 'Company!'

The restaurant of the Chateau Strain was a charming room done in red and gold with a splendid view of Stone harbour, full of people eating bits of fish piled up into towers with various vegetables. As the Ghost kicked the door open, the restaurant became full of people with open mouths and eyes bulging out of their heads. As the two-metre skeleton with red hair, lizardskin cowboy boots and a fried shroud strode across the carpet dripping boiling oil, the restaurant became full of people stampeding for the door.

The only person who did not stampede was a very fat man at a table by the window. This was partly because his little black eyes were fixed on the monstrous array of dishes in front of him, and partly because he was wedged in.

The Ghost marched over to him, pulled out a chair and sat down. 'Any good?' he said.

The fat man did not look up. He was stuffing a shrimp into his mouth and scribbling in a notebook headed GOLDEN MEATBALL AWARD – NOTES. 'It's all mine,' he said. 'You can't have any.'

'Aaaah,' said the Ghost. 'C'm*on*.' He reached out a bony hand and grasped a whole cod decorated with green bits. Holding the cod by the tail, he raised it above his head and lowered it into his fleshless jaws. There was a splat as the fish fell out of the bottom of his ribcage. 'Mm,' he said. '*Delicious.*'

It was at this point that the fat man looked up.

'AIEEE,' cried the fat man, and leaped to his feet.

When someone that fat leaps, everything around him tends to leap with him. The table shot in the air. So did the twenty-eight plates, bowls, dishes and tureens that covered it. The Ghost raised his arms and said, 'WOO'.

The fat man lurched backwards against the picture window. The window bulged outwards and shattered into 10,731 pieces.

'GRAAAAA,' howled the fat man, falling outwards.

'SPLASH,' said the harbour.

'What's the water like?' cried the Ghost, leaning out and dripping hot oil.

There was a crunch and a roar as the Stone lifeboat shot down the launch ramp and arrived alongside the inspector.

Alfie Tank was leaning over the side. 'I am sooo sorry!' he cried.

'Appalling!' cried the inspector. 'It stole my food! The scallops were overdone! The mayonnaise lacked creaminess! I shall remove your stars!'

'Eeeeh!' cried Tank. 'Nooo!'

'Yes!' cried the inspector.

'Rrh,' said Tank, in a small but penetrating voice much more worrying than the one he used for cursing and swearing. 'Just *wait* till I get my hands on that frying chef!'

The words travelled in at the window and arrived at the swing door into the kitchen, where Buddy and Lou were standing one either side of Kenyatta. Kenyatta had his face in his hands.

'I think he means you,' said Buddy.

'What do you think he'll do?' said Lou.

'Help me!' said Kenyatta.

'Certainly,' said Lou. 'Enid?'

Enid strode into the restaurant. Below the

window, the lifeboat men were trying to haul the fat inspector on to the boat while Alfie Tank was trying to throw him back into the harbour before he could write his report.

'Ho, ho, ho,' said the Ghost.

'Box time, Bones,' said Enid.

'But I want to see what happens!'

'*In*,' said Enid, snapping open the lid of the porcelain snuffbox.

'All right, all *right*,' said the Ghost. 'Com*ing*.'

He vanished into the box like a stream of batter from a spoon. Enid stuffed him into her hip pocket and marched out to the limo. They hid Kenyatta in the boot, put the snuffbox in the glove compartment and sped back towards Castle Bones.

As they crossed the hills into the valley of the Dusk and the lights of Smoke City lay spread across the dark land ahead, noises started to come from the glove compartment: a rattling, and a grunting, and once a high, clear shriek that said, 'MY TURN SOON.'

'Well, we owe him one,' said Buddy.

'Two, in fact,' said Lou.

5

Kenyatta and Fingers Trubshaw slept in the Recovery Suite. Both of them woke up screaming several times, but that (said Lou to Buddy, who agreed) was only to be expected. The children took them breakfast next day sharp at 4 p.m. First on the trolley list was Fingers.

'Coffee?' said Lou, pouring a pint mug. 'Oo, it's a bit strong.' She fixed an eye on the bassist's sleepy countenance. 'Pitch-black, actually.'

Except she did not get the 'actually' out. Because

at the sound of the word 'pitch', Fingers Trubshaw had leaped out of bed, lime-green flannel pyjamas and all, and was on top of the wardrobe gibbering and trying to pull his hair out by the roots.

'By the way,' said Lou, the picture of elegance in her wine-red blazer and box-pleat skirt. 'There are some people from the World Cricket Wicket Association on the phone. I –'

'Mmmmew,' said Fingers, gibbering a bit more.

'As I was saying. I told them you are mowing in the Far East for the next few years.' With an elegant flourish, Lou whipped a silver cover off a plate. 'Now then. Come on down and have your bacon and eggs. You are quite safe here.'

'Thank you,' said Fingers, falling off the wardrobe in his gratitude. 'Thank you, *thank* you!'

Lou backed out of the room. 'Band meeting at eight, Hall of Columns,' she said.

It was all going awfully well.

Buddy took the trolley over from his sister and shoved it along to Kenyatta's door. The only part of the drummer visible above the duvet was his tam-o'-shanter.

'Ahoy!' cried Buddy. 'Yoo-hoo! Show a leg! Breakfast!'

He poured a pint mug of strong cocoa, which he knew of old was Kenyatta's favourite breakfast drink, and wafted the smell of the cup across to him with a page of sheet music.

The duvet came down. One eye appeared above it, and a set of nostrils, twitching.

'Cocoa,' said Kenyatta. 'Mm.'

'And afterwards,' said Buddy, 'how about a few fried eggs and a spot of bacon?'

At least, that was what he meant to say. Actually he only got as far as the word 'fried' when Kenyatta rocketed straight upward and came to rest on the chandelier, gibbering with terror and dressed only in the tam-o'-shanter and a blood-red flannel nightshirt.

'Oh, yes,' said Buddy, arranging a plateful of poached eggs on toast on the bedside table. 'There was some geezer on the phone who said his name was Harry Bus, tell a lie, Alfie Tank, and he wanted to see you. But we thought you wouldn't want to see him. So we told him you have gone stunt-frying in the Southern Continent and will be impossible to contact.'

'Thank you,' said Kenyatta, lowering himself from the chandelier. 'Thank you, *thank* you!'

'Don't mention it,' said Buddy. 'Oh, by the way, band meeting at eight in the Hall of Columns. OK?'

Kenyatta closed his eyes. He could still see the raging face of Alfie Tank. Last night it had been so close he could have touched it. Today it was smaller, and on the other side of a line of roadies. Big roadies, with linked arms, guarding the high, high walls of Castle Bones. Walls so high that nobody as fat as Tank could climb them in a million years.

'I'll be there,' he said, and tucked into the eggs.

Buddy slid out of the room.

It was going awfully well.

Or so he thought. But he was forgetting one thing. You can get your rock star in your castle. But you can't make him punctual.

Buddy was forgetting this.

But Vlad wasn't.

The Hall of Columns was ready for business. In the clearing by the toad pool, a long table bore dozens of glittering candles. There were four places, each with jug of water, writing pad and pencils freshly sharpened. As the stroke of eight boomed through the castle, a door opened and closed somewhere in the shadows. A dark figure glided between the pale columns of marble, handed its cloak to a waiting roadie, sat down and looked at its watch, an elaborate affair with a matt-black face and a razor-sharp pendulum.

'Vell?' said the figure. 'Vere is everyone?'

'Late, Vlad,' said the roadie from the darkness.

'The meeting is for eight,' said Vlad.

'Yeah, but this is rock and roll.'

Vlad flicked a speck of bat dung from his perfect cuff. 'No matter,' he said. 'A meeting is a meeting.' He pulled a piece of paper from his black human-skin briefcase. 'Now. Item I. Musical policy of Death Eric. Will change to include Whirl Music as of now. Votes?' He looked at the empty chairs down the table. 'Comments und remarks? No? OK, we vote. I vote yes. Objections?'

Silence, except for the sound of a large throat being cleared in a small way.

'Vlad?' said the adoring voice of Enid.

'Ja?' said Vlad, impatiently.

'It is, like, usual to wait for the others. You've got

away with this once. You won't get away with it a second time.'

'Hah!' said Vlad, fixing her with his deep black eyes. 'Where I come from, what is usual is to be efficient.'

'Yes, Vlad,' said Enid. She had a vague feeling that she had been about to argue or something . . .

Vlad blinked.

She nearly passed out.

Vlad opened his eyes.

She fell in, like a roadie falling down a well.

'Yes,' she said.

'Yes what?'

'Yes whatever, Vlad.'

'Yeah,' said Vlad. 'So now we have a music policy. And we go into the studio. Tonight. With the New Look.'

'Tonight wha?' said a voice from the shadows.

'Recording, Eric,' said Vlad. 'You are late.'

'Late? Oof,' said Eric, colliding with a column. 'Sorry, man. Hey! Fingers! That you?'

'Who wants to know?' said Fingers' voice from elsewhere in the gloom.

'Me. Eric. I think,' said Eric, losing confidence.

'Who's there?' said another voice, very shaky.

'Fingers and Eric, Kenyatta,' said Enid.

'Guys!' cried Eric. 'Great to see you! Except I can't.'

'Oh,' said Kenyatta, relieved.

'Oh,' said Fingers, relieved too.

'Wo,' said Eric. 'Me bat's gone.'

'Bat?' said Fingers, made nervous by this mention of cricket equipment.

'Relax, everyone,' said Enid. 'Just sit down and we will start again and have a vote on Music Policy and then we can all go quad biking in the woods.'

'We don't need to vote,' said Fingers.

'We know what we play,' said Kenyatta.

'Music,' said Eric.

'Feedback metal music,' said Kenyatta.

'Nyet,' said Vlad.

'And who,' said Fingers, 'are you?'

'Which is what I wanna know too,' said Kenyatta.

'I am Vlad,' said Vlad, lighting a cigarette and blowing a horrible cloud. 'From now on so-called Death Eric has New Look, playink Whirl Music supporting Honganian Folk Orchestra. Vill bring music to new audience und move band to next level. Vote has been taken as per constitution.'

His gaze fell on Enid.

'Yes,' said Enid, in the voice of a huge but beautiful Love Robot.

'Folk?' said Fingers, horrified.

'Orchestra?' said Kenyatta, stunned.

'Pies?' said Eric, unnerved.

'Nobody has mentioned pies.'

'They will,' said Eric gloomily. 'Heavy ones, no beans.'

'For supper, ja,' said Vlad. 'Meeting over, then.' He rose and glided off between the columns.

'*Well,*' said Enid, with rather forced cheerfulness. 'Nice to have someone in charge, eh, guys?'

'No,' said Fingers.

'No,' said Kenyatta.

'Me bat,' said Eric.

'Supper in twenty minutes,' said Enid. 'And after, why don't you have a little play?'

She had a nasty feeling, and it went like this. It was just as well she and the road crew were the only thing standing between her band and long prison sentences. Otherwise they would have gone home. She had the feeling that the band were not happy with their musical direction. And she had the oddest feeling that some of it was her fault . . .

Still, they had Vlad. *Strong* management. Oo,

nice, thought Enid, tumbling back into her warm pink Love Trance.

The studio was a large crypt studded with fat columns like stone tree trunks. There was a sort of clearing in front of the control-room window. In the clearing, the roadies had put up the gear. Kenyatta McClatter's drums were in the middle, the cymbals hovering like flying saucers round the space station of toms, snare and bass drum. On the left was Fingers Trubshaw's custom Wheel Horse bass stack. (Wheel Horse normally make motor mowers, but as Fingers always said, a reliable lawn-mower and a reliable bass stack are just about the same thing. When you are famous you can talk any old rubbish and no one will argue.) And on the right were the eight cabs and four linked tops of Eric Thrashmettle's legendary –

Cabs? Tops?

Sorry. For those who do not already know, cabs are what roadies call speaker cabinets. Tops are the amplifier bits that sit on top of them, with knobs that you twiddle to turn the volume up from very very loud to very very loud indeed.

– Eric Thrashmettle's legendary rig. To which

was attached by an armoured lead his heavy-duty pedal, with the footswitch outlined in red neon and bearing the words TREAD HERE in case of mistakes. To which was attached by another heavy-duty cable Eric's legendary guitar Rabid Dingo, the matt-black Gibson Flying V, heavily toothmarked.

Kenyatta sat down behind his drums, picked up the sticks and started a little thumpa thumpa thumpa beat. Lounging on the velvet sofa in the control room, Lou was surprised to feel her toes twitching, and to see the reflections in her brother's perfectly polished shoes distorting as his own toes performed a small private boogie. Fingers Trubshaw picked his gleaming red Fender Precision bass off its stand, ducked into the strap, flicked the STANDBY switch, and started a doowop oppa boppa figure across Kenyatta's thumpa thumpa thumpa. Buddy felt his foot begin to tap, and was surprised to see his sister's knee moving faintly under her perfectly ironed skirt. The slight gloom cast by Vlad began to lift.

Eric picked up Rabid Dingo, strapped it on, and waved his arms around in a baffled manner. A small roadie went out and took the guitar off him and put it on the other way round.

'You're right-handed,' said the roadie. 'Not left-handed.'

'Am I?' said Eric. His knees were flexing slightly to the rhythm section's groove. He pulled a pick out of the Baron Samedi Souvenir of Haiti human ear pick holder on Rabid Dingo's tailfin. His trainer crawled across the floor like a small, filthy animal, found the pedal and pushed down.

Somewhere in outer space a chainsaw started up. It flew closer, howled through the props of an enormous building made of steel and wood and glass. The building shuddered, then collapsed with a giant roar. As it went down, hundreds of angels soared from the ruins, uttering songs of perfect sweetness in piercing harmony, and flew towards the sunset, where they were joined by several million more angels flying personal jets and singing a big roaring freight-train rhythm that was quite definitely the introduction to –

'"Pig Train"!' cried Lou, clapping her hands.

'Good old Dad!' cried Buddy, banging his head.

Then all they could do was clap hands and bang heads. Because Death Eric were back, and playing, and playing really really well, and they were not even warmed up yet –

'No,' said an enormous voice. 'No, no, *no*, NO, NO!' A pale hand pulled a plug out of a wall. The guitars ceased, and Kenyatta stopped drumming. In the middle of the studio, plug in hand, stood Vlad.

'NO!' he cried. 'Is not good! Is old stupid music, no place for excellent ood and skveezebox New Look.'

'Oh,' said Fingers.

'Oh,' said Kenyatta.

'It was here somewhere,' said Eric. 'Me bat, like.'

'Your bat is not important,' said Vlad.

There was a short but well-stuffed silence. Nobody spoke to Eric like this, not with Enid in the room anyway. Not unless he wanted to leave on a stretcher.

'Wha,' said Eric.

'Forget about your bat,' said Enid.

Vlad's eyes were on her. She was speaking in a strange, tinny voice. There was a look on her face as if she was trapped in an awful dream. Lou went across the room, planning to hold her hand. Buddy opened his mouth to ask Vlad who he thought he was talking to.

'Oh,' said Eric, who as far as anyone could tell

trusted Enid more than he trusted himself. 'Whatever. Guys?'

'Yeah, well, oods,' said Fingers, reminded of cricket grounds by this talk of bats. 'Try anything once.'

'It's a free country,' said Kenyatta, chasing from his head the memory of fat mauve Alfie Tank and substituting a small wait-and-see paradiddle.

'OK,' said Eric.

Vlad gave a short, curt nod. Various small Honganians began to grin among the columns, hovering over instruments made of elk guts and wolves' teeth.

'"Happy Peasants Rejoice in the Arrival of Mobile Dentist's Van". Slobodna brodnye!' cried Vlad. '– a-FOUR!'

The racket began.

It was unspeakable. Normally Enid would have stopped it. Now she was staring at Vlad, glassy-eyed.

Buddy caught Lou's eye. They went into the control room.

Buddy said, 'This is horrible.'

'Dad'll fire Vlad at the end of the song,' said Lou. 'Poor Enid!'

They watched the musicians. Death Eric looked miserable. The Honganians looked madly excited. The music sounded like wildebeests migrating through china shops. After about six months the last savannah creature strolled through the last tea set and the last Honganian folk dancer leaped vertically in the air, stunned himself on the ceiling and fell senseless to the floor. A gloomy silence descended.

'Bravo!' cried Vlad, clapping.

'Rubbish,' said Eric.

Lou took hold of Buddy's hand and gave it a squeeze, as if to say, Here we go. Then her grip tightened and grew clammy.

Enid shook her head as if awaking from sleep. She started to look stern and resolute. She opened her mouth to tell all the Honganians to get out of the studio before everyone had freak accidents one after another. Then she caught Vlad's eye. And she simpered and went pink and glassy again and said, 'That was very nice.'

Eric's mouth fell open. 'Wha?' he said.

'Next!' said Vlad.

Roadies carried the stunned dancers out on planks and brought in new ones. 'Slobodna brodnye!' cried one and all. 'Next tune: "Women of Brsmsk Are Joyfully Scrubbing Sewers, Polka". A-vun –'

'Come,' said Lou. Noses high, she and Buddy stalked from the studio. And they did not stop stalking until they were at the Gothic cottage.

There were no words. There was only the familiar feel of the piano keyboard under Buddy's fingers, and the cello neck in Lou's hand, and the calm logic of Lupp's Soft Music for a Hard Time. Soon, the frightful racket they had just heard was a faint, grim memory.

'So,' said Lou, after the piece had moved through four keys, modulated into the relative minor and resolved with a triumphant return to the main theme. 'Where do we go from here?'

'We stick stamps on these idiots and post them straight back to Hongania,' said Buddy.

'Be sensible,' said Lou, drumming her fingers on the cello. 'That awful Vlad has got poor Enid completely hypnotized. We've got to get rid of him.'

Buddy played the theme from *Hang 'em High*. 'He's going to be hard to shift,' he said. 'I mean, his eyes . . .'

'Strong personality,' said Lou. 'Yes indeed. So apple-pie beds, all that, no good. The band won't throw him out because Enid won't say boo to him and Dad'll do what Enid says and the others think they'll get arrested –'

'Quite rightly,' said Buddy.

'– as soon as they go out of the gate. So we've got a brilliant band playing dreadful music with two weeks to go before the next album has to be delivered to the recording company, New Look and all. And I am twelve and you are eleven. What do we do?'

'It's obvious,' said Buddy.

'Of course it is,' said Lou.

'We talk to the Ghost,' they said, both together.

There was a silence. 'But what do we *say* to him?' said Buddy.

'Leave that to me,' said Lou.

So at ten past two, there they were in the Library.

'Take it away, bro,' said Lou.

Buddy sat down at the harpsichord and began to hammer out 'Bad Skoool', playing an E major chord instead of an E minor chord in the chorus. There was a disgusting smell, a roll of thunder, a sudden chill, and the Ghost was in their midst.

'You're playing a wrong *chord*!' it said pettishly. 'I *told* you!'

'It's a great song,' said Lou hurriedly. 'Really great. It doesn't get nearly enough airplay nowadays.'

'Yeah,' said the Ghost, shaking its skull gloomily. 'If you don't get radio, you're dead.'

'Too true,' said Buddy cleverly.

'What I need,' said the ghost of Aluminium Dave, 'is someone to cover it.'

'Oh?'

'Someone,' said the Ghost, 'like Death Eric.'

'Mm,' said Lou. 'Do you know, I think that could maybe be arranged? Seeing as we owe you a favour anyway.'

'It could?' said the Ghost, looking as eager as it is possible for a wormy old skull to look.

'On certain conditions,' said Buddy.

'Conditions?' said the Ghost, in a voice like the slam of a crypt door.

'There is this bloke Vlad,' said Buddy. 'And a bunch of Honganians. We want them out of here. To show you're serious.'

'I dunno,' said the Ghost, who seemed to be getting more rock and roll by the minute. 'I mean it's not really a ghost's job. More a job for a manager.'

'Like you've totally got a manager,' said Buddy rather sharply.

'Ahem,' said Lou, cutting her brother off. 'It was just that we really love and admire your records and would really like to hear more of them and also your style at the Cricket Ground and the Sea Food Restaurant was, well, something else.' She kicked Buddy sharply under the table. 'Eh, Buddy?'

'Ow,' said Buddy. 'I mean oh. Yes. Far, er, out. Wouldn't be surprised if someone heard the cover and decided to sign you again.'

'If you can get Death Eric to do the cover,' said Lou. 'Which you won't if the Honganians are still here.'

'Mm,' said the Ghost. It brightened, in a bony sort of way. 'All right,' it said. 'I'll do what I can.'

Vlad was a fussy dresser. As the sun went down the next night he rose, yawned, stretched and shrugged into a shirt of finest chamois leather. He pulled on his lizardskin trousers and sat down in front of his mirror. Picking up a small pair of tweezers, he began the delicate task of reshaping the right-hand end of his left eyebrow.

'You are sooo lovely,' he told himself.

Someone sat down on his dressing-table stool.

'Human life is short,' said a voice next to him. 'Beauty passes.'

'Not mine,' said Vlad. 'And who's human, anyway? Now, do you mind not interrupting while I am talking to myself?'

'Repent!' cried a voice like a piano falling down a coal mine.

Vlad frowned. He could see his own exquisite self in the mirror. (Mirrors are a problem for vain vampires, who, as everyone knows, have no reflection. Vlad solved it by eating pies as well as blood, which gave him a slightly hazy look, but good enough for personal grooming.) But whatever was sitting beside him did not seem to have any reflection at all. Drat these supernaturals, he thought. Much more of this and his eyebrow-care programme would be disrupted.

'Listen,' he said. 'What I can't see in the mirror can't hurt me. So could you put a sock in it?'

'At Castle Bones, madness stalks the corridors,' said the voice. Then it laughed, a fearsome peal accompanied by thunder and lightning.

'Oh for goodness' *sake*,' said Vlad. He turned on his seat. As he had expected, next to him was a horrid greenish sack of slime with red eyes, gnashing hundreds of teeth. 'You may not care what you look like,' he said, 'but a manager has to make a good impression. Groomink,' said Vlad, 'is crucial.'

The Ghost produced a dagger and stabbed itself several times in the eyeball. He had done this to Boris Batter, drummer of Pinhead, when Pinhead were making their thrash album *Ballet Shoes* at Castle Bones. Boris had screamed and screamed and for all anyone knew was still screaming, though it was hard to tell because of the soundproof padding in his cell.

Vlad said, 'Ghostski, if you do not put that knife down you vill cut somebody. Now, if you vill excuse me, I have some pies to eat and lovely ood music to arrange.'

Flinging his black cloak about his shoulders, he swept from the room.

'Drat,' said the Ghost. It shrank into a pool of green slime and evaporated.

Buddy and Lou were in the studio when Vlad came in.

'Goodness!' said Lou. 'You look as if you've seen a ghost!'

Vlad smoothed one eyebrow with a finger. 'And the Ghost saw me,' he said. 'Score: Vlad vun, Ghost nil.'

'Oo,' breathed Enid. 'He's so *brave*.'

'I may vomit,' said Lou, making a fake retching noise.

'Now!' cried Vlad. 'Come, my fiery companions of steppe and mountain! Grab your oods and skveezeboxes, and away! Slobodna brodnye! Vun two THREE!'

And up the dismal racket started again.

'Back to the drawing board,' said Lou.

As they walked through the Hall of Columns, a telephone was ringing.

'Won't be anything important,' said Sid the Soothsayer, who was tending a small, unusual-smelling fire by the toad pool.

Naturally, Buddy picked the phone up.

'Yeah,' said the voice at the far end. 'Whozat?'

'Death Eric management,' said Buddy cagily.

'Yeah,' said the voice at the far end. It was slow and distant and sounded as if it was used to being listened to. 'This is your record company speaking. I am Running Dave the A&R man, man.'

'Yeah?' said Buddy coolly, though actually he

was a bit awestruck. Running Dave was a really exceptionally chilled person. A&R stood for Artists and Repertoire. This meant that Running Dave was the man who said Death Eric were brilliant or past it. Running Dave, in fact, was the Man with the Power. And he was a full-blooded Cherokee Indian by adoption. And he wore a remarkably cool suit. 'It's happening,' said Buddy. 'Man.'

'I wanna hear the new act, see how the New Look's going,' said Running Dave. 'I thought, why not arrange a gig at the El Blotto? See how it's all coming together.'

'Ah,' said Buddy. A film had suddenly started running in his head. The El Blotto Tea Rooms was Smoke City's most exclusive intimate nightclub-type venue. In Buddy's mind, the stage was full of tone-deaf Honganian midgets in fur hats. And the air was full of brickbats, shoes and rotten vegetables. And the newspapers were full of headlines that said things like IMAGINE THE WORST GIG EVER – NOW DOUBLE THAT. 'Yeeah,' he said. 'I think Eric may be coming down with, er, flu –'

'I'll send a doctor,' said Running Dave. 'Friday

night all right? The band'll be glad to take some time out of the studio, I expect.'

From the lower reaches of Castle Bones came the sound of Honganian instruments under heavy torture.

'Yes,' said Buddy. 'They probably will.'

The telephone went down.

'Oops,' said Lou, when Buddy told her. 'This needs careful thought. They can't possibly play –'

'Who can't possibly play?' said a smooth voice very close at hand.

'Yaroo!' cried Buddy, shocked.

'Eeek!' cried Lou, surprised.

'Deed I starrrtle you?' said Vlad, stepping out of the shadows. 'How very wonderful. A gig, I hear. And in the El Blotto Tea Rooms. What a treat for the audience.'

'Perhaps,' said Lou. 'But do you think the world is *ready* for Whirl Music?'

'Slobodna brodnye!' cried Vlad, his eyes blazing. 'Hongania is a great country and all peoples of mind and soul admit this! Now, I must go to my lads and tell them I have got them a gig!'

'*You* got them a gig?' said Buddy. 'It was –'

But Vlad had already swept away.

'Obviously he doesn't mind ghosts,' said Buddy. 'Well, we'll fix him another way.'

'Like how?'

'We'll think of something.'

But actually, neither of them believed it.

It was a grim evening. The pies at supper were extra heavy. Kenyatta played a tune on his with his knife and fork before pushing it away untouched. Fingers squinted at his from all directions, then rolled it into the shadows, where it stunned a rat. But Buddy and Lou were hungry, so they ate. And after supper they went to the Gothic cottage and played music. But even Eno's Digestive Suite could not rid them of the gloom and the stomach ache.

'Groo,' said Buddy, pushing himself away from the keyboard. 'I'm off to bed.'

'Me too,' said Lou, laying down her cello. Together they walked back to the castle. Castle Bones sprawled under the moon like a huge dead animal. And from the direction of the recording studio, tinny and awful, came the sound of Honganian music.

'Groo,' said Buddy again.

'Night, then,' said Lou.

She went to bed. But she did not sleep.

She counted sheep.

She counted goats, ants and stars.

The great clock struck ten and eleven.

The pain in her stomach did not abate.

Finally she could stand it no longer. Swinging her feet out of bed, she put on a brocade dressing gown and padded down the icy stone stairs, heading for the Roadies' Wing, where Enid slept in her enormous bed by her enormous medicine cupboard, which would contain at least three flavours of fizzy indigestion drink.

The way took her through the Long Long Gallery, which (as its name suggests) was very very long. As she came to the beginning of the gallery, Lou paused.

The gallery had windows all down one side. Opposite the windows was a wall of pictures, mostly of twisted old noblefolk. At the far end, a twenty-metre space had been reserved for gold discs won by bands who had made their records at Castle Bones.

Bong, said the castle clock, sounding the first stroke of midnight. Starlight was seeping in through the windows, bathing the gallery in a faint bluish glow. At the far end, where the gold discs hung, there was an odd, semi-transparent commotion.

A tall figure in a luminous bluish-green gown was scrabbling at the wall with fingers of naked bone. It seemed to be grasping gold discs, shouting at them, and throwing them out of the window. Cautiously, Lou crept closer.

It was the Ghost, of course. She hid behind a suit of armour and watched him read the label on a disc.

'Rubbish!' he cried. 'Copycats!' He hurled the record out of the window and gripped another. 'Honganian drivel!' he cried. 'Atrocious!' Hurl. Seize another. 'Awful!' he cried. 'Who did they bribe to get that into the Top Ten?' Hurl. Crash. 'And now I must *plead* to get my songs played!' Fling. Splinter.

'Ahem,' said Lou. 'Can I help at all?'

'Do me a favour,' said the Ghost, holding out a gleaming platter in the fitful starlight. 'Dark Albert and the Sons of Squeeze *Black Mass at Midnite*. What, I ask you, does Dark Albert know about black masses? He's tucked up with his *teddies* by nine! Graaah!'

With this cry of other-worldly disgust, the Ghost hurled the gold disc out of the window.

Lou sat down in a heavily carved chair. She said, 'Ghost, I think you are unhappy.'

'Unhappy? You try being a ghost,' said the Ghost.

'Why,' said Lou, 'do you not sit down and tell me about it?'

The Ghost stared at her. 'I am a rocker, not a whinger,' he said.

'Everyone needs to share,' said Lou.

'Sigh,' said the Ghost, as well as someone can who has got no lungs. 'You are a very nice person for an Exister, did you know that?'

'One does one's best,' said Lou. 'Now, then. Tell me everything.'

'It's got grim bits,' said the Ghost.

'Grim bits and all,' said Lou.

'OK,' said the Ghost. He shook his head. 'I am tired, so tired. I have not slept for thirty-five years.'

'Are you by any chance related to Keith Richards of the Rolling Stones?'

'Who?'

'Forget it,' said Lou. 'How did it begin?'

'Well, you know, there was that business with the Transformer Lake. I don't remember it very well. I went diving all right. Then there is a sort of bit of a blackout, like being on stage, lights in your eyes and everything. And then like here I am in the old castle. And I don't know how I know it, but I do know it, that every day I have to turn the water in that cauldron into blood –'

'– or my Wizzo Bath Salts,' said Lou. 'I got them for Christmas. And they're mauve, not red.'

'Oh, yeah, so you'd rather I found real blood somewhere?' said the Ghost.

Lou bowed. 'I stand corrected,' she said. 'Proceed.'

'It's all part of the Curse of Castle Bones. One, cauldron into blood,' said the Ghost, ticking off the haunt menu on his pure bone fingers. 'Two, stalk Long Long Gallery at midnight hour. Three, perform extra hauntings whenever possible, but limited to castle except when snuffboxed.'

'That's it?'

'That's it.'

'Not much of a life,' said Lou.

'A life,' said the Ghost, 'is exactly what it is not.'

'Sorry,' said Lou, feeling that she had rather put her foot in it.

'Granted.'

'So how,' said Lou, 'can you escape this . . . er . . .'

'Routine is the best word,' said the Ghost. 'By doing certain things. But I don't know what they all are.'

'Why don't we help you find out?'

'Because you're children.'

'We are not normal children,' said Lou. 'Few children are, of course. But our great good luck is that we have been brought up in the world of Rock and Roll, where anything can happen. So explain, and I will see what we can do. If anything,' she added fair-mindedly.

'OK. Like I said,' said the Ghost, 'I'm sick of haunting. I want to stop.'

'So tell me these certain things,' said Lou.

'One, I've got to become world famous again.'

'Hmm,' said Lou. In her view, a two-metre skeleton with walking eyeballs and lizardskin cowboy boots would not find world fame hard to come by. 'And?'

'The world fame isn't exactly a condition,' said the Ghost. 'More a personal goal, really. The actual conditions laid down by, I dunno, the Keeper of the Castle Bones Curse or someone, are somewhere on the master copy of *Red Meat Pomeroy*. And actually apparently they lift the Castle Bones Curse too.'

'What's *Red Meat Pomeroy*?'

'The album we were mixing when I . . . when the accident happened.'

'So play it, what's stopping you?'

The Ghost looked shifty. 'Don't know where it is.'

'You mean you've lost it.'

'It used to be here on the wall with all the gold discs,' said the Ghost. 'As recently as ten years ago. But it seems to have gone. And I want it back.'

Lou tapped a disapproving foot. 'You mean it's been hanging here for thirty-five years and you've never *played* it?'

'I can't,' said the Ghost. 'Not allowed. It's in the rules.'

'What rules?'

The Ghost looked as worried as a mouldering skull can look, which is actually not all that worried. 'The Curse. Apparently a pure, innocent, kind person without spot or stain has to play the record to me, and you don't get many of them round metal recording studios. But I think maybe you're one. Only the record's vanished. So what would be great,' said the Ghost, 'is if you could sort of have a look for it? And play it if you find it? You'll like it. It's brilliant,' said the Ghost modestly.

'Of course I will,' said Lou, who was actually rather flattered by all this. 'Buddy and I will look first thing tomorrow. Plus,' she said, 'tomorrow there is a gig at the El Blotto Tea Rooms. Which, come to think of it, is actually the ideal moment to start you back on the road to world fame.'

'Oh, goodie!' cried the Ghost, with a whimsical crash of thunder. 'I can't wait!'

He vanished, nicely, with no smell.

Lou took herself off to bed. Her indigestion had totally gone.

And unless she was much mistaken, Death Eric's New Look had totally arrived.

6

Next morning at the weirdly early hour of eleven o'clock the band were gathered round the breakfast table arguing about the set list for the El Blotto Tea Rooms gig.

'Old favourites,' said Fingers. 'Can't beat 'em.'

'Yeah,' said Kenyatta. 'It'll whet their appetite.'

'Wet what?' said Eric, his mouth full of muesli.

'And Honganian Whirl Music laterr,' said Vlad.

'Old faves will be lovely,' said Enid, smiling the smile of an ape with someone standing on its foot. She caught Vlad's eye and her mind went squashy. 'And a tiny bit of Honganian stuff? To please me?'

Fingers and Kenyatta looked at Eric as if they hoped he would say something. But Eric was looking deep into his muesli.

'I'm sure something like stirred in there,' he said.

Lou said, 'You know what would be really nice, now we're at Castle Bones? To play that old Aluminium Dave Krang number.'

'Wha?'

'"Bad Skoool",' said Buddy.

'Great tune,' said Eric.

'Why not?' said Kenyatta.

'We could fit it in somewhere,' said Fingers.

'Heh, heh,' said Buddy. He rose. So did Lou.

'Excuse me,' they said politely, and left.

They sat in the glow of the stained-glass window in the library. Lou explained what the Ghost had told her.

'It is a sad tale,' she said. 'We must make certain that this poor wandering spirit can rest.'

'Oh totally,' said Buddy. 'So all we've got to do is make it world famous and find some record it made. Which could be anywhere.'

'Use your head,' said Lou. 'What happens to a record on a recording studio wall?'

'The next band pulls it off the wall and throws it out of the window.'

'Yea, verily!' cried Lou, clapping her hands.

'What?' said Buddy.

'Come!' she cried, and dragged her brother out of the front door and across the dank garden. 'Here!' she cried, indicating a tall, rubbish-heap-like mound.

'But it's a rubbish heap.'

'Exactly.'

'Wha.'

Lou pointed a quivering finger at a line of windows that crossed the huge side of the castle three floors above the rubbish heap.

'The Long Long Gallery,' she said. 'Dig!'

'Gosh,' said Buddy, forgetting his best shoes and his finest designer trousers and plunging into the rubbish heap. 'You're right!'

They began to dig.

Reader, jealousy is a terrible thing, and nowhere is it more terrible than in the world of feedback metal. Generations of recording artistes had recorded gold discs at Castle Bones. Next generations had thrown the last generation's discs out of the window, only to have their own discs thrown out in turn. The two-metre mound in front of Buddy and Lou was basically a mound of gold discs, sandwiched between layers of discarded lawn-mowings.

'Gosh!' cried Buddy, holding up a disc. '*Pig Train!*'

'Save it for Dad. A reminder of the good old days.'

'Before Vlad,' said Buddy. 'If Running Dave hears this Whirl Music rubbish –'

'That's taken care of,' said Lou. 'Dig!'

They dug. They dug through thirty-one years of musical history. The lawnmowings became slime, then dust. But the gold discs gleamed brightly, their labels as good as new, thanks to the enduring power of the precious metal. (Yes, yes, gold discs are actually gold-plated, everyone knows that. But these ones were real gold. It is not called feedback *metal* for nothing.)

Finally, Buddy said, 'Oi!'

'Wha?'

There was a disc in his hand. It was not gold but black. Buddy squinted at the label.

'"*Red Meat Pomeroy*",' he said, '"by Aluminium

Dave Krang. The Original Master Acetate", it says here, which I can tell you, dear sister, is a kind of old-fashioned template for a vinyl album. "Framed by his Friends to Commemorate his Tragic Disappearance."'

'Game on!' said Lou.

'Upstairs!' said Buddy.

Buddy had assembled his sound system himself. It was very large and very complicated, capable of playing anything from advanced-format MP3s to ancient wax cylinders. He put the acetate disc through a vacuum washer, laid it carefully on the turntable, turned on a small oil nozzle to mute the hiss and crackle, and lowered the stylus.

'Cans,' he said, handing Lou a pair of enormous headphones and clamping a set on his own head.

Lou settled back in a chair to listen.

Aluminium Dave played perfectly acceptable early-seventies metal music. The guitars were primitive, the vocals gave you a sore throat just to hear them, and the drum solo was mercifully short. Buddy played side one. Then he played side two. Then he engaged a battery of oscilloscopes, sound analysers and frequency logs. Then he did it all again.

Finally Buddy took his cans off (Lou had removed hers some time previously). 'If there's a message in there,' he said, 'it is very, very well hidden.'

'Or not there at all.'

From below there came the sound of swearing. When Buddy looked out of the window he saw roadies loading gear into the back of a small fleet of vans ready for the El Blotto Tea Rooms gig.

'They'll be off in half an hour,' said Lou. 'We'd better get that ghost into that snuff box.'

'So what do you think will happen?' said Buddy.

'Who knows? But,' said Lou, 'the Ghost wants World Fame. And he will not let Whirl Music get in his way. So you can bet it will be something.'

'I see what you mean,' said Buddy.

The El Blotto Tea Rooms was an enormous cellar full of little tables and comfortable chairs upholstered in red velvet. There was a stage at one end, a door at the other, and various small candlelit alcoves. It looked more like a place for tired businessmen than a metal venue, but the biggest bands in the universe (simple folk at heart) loved it because you got very good food and a nice big dressing room.

Not that the dressing room felt very big tonight.

Buddy and Lou were in there, of course. So was Kenyatta, frying a slab of cod in a portable fat vat, and Fingers, whispering sweet nothings to a rose bush that was sickening for something. Eric was leaning his head against the wall, watching an ant that was coming out of a crack in the plaster, walking across the wall and disappearing into another crack. He had been trying to train it for ten minutes. Originally he had assumed it was one ant, going round in a circle. Now he was beginning to wonder whether it was actually quite a lot of ants, one after the other, in which case the training presented pretty enormous problems.

'One ant is very like another,' he said.

Everyone ignored him, or maybe they did not hear, because the rest of the dressing room was full of chattering Honganians. Pies surged across the room like frisbees, and every now and then someone toasted someone else in sour milk. Someone was tuning a zither, and someone else was tuning an ood, and neither was in tune with the other. The noise was frightful.

Buddy touched the snuffbox in his pocket. It felt strangely cold. 'If anyone wants us, we'll be out front,' he said.

'Nice one,' said Enid, patting him vaguely on the head. She was gazing with adoring eyes at Vlad, who was saying something masterful to a skveeze-box player.

Front of house was filling up. Waiters in black uniforms scurried among the tables carrying champagne bottles on trays. The biggest table of all was the record company table. There were many executives with fat cigars and glossy hairdos. At the head of the table, cool as a medium-sized iceberg in shades (of which Buddy approved) and a turquoise string tie (of which Buddy did not) sat Running Dave. Next to him, beautiful as a New Mexico dawn in snow-white fringed doeskin, sat his girlfriend, C&W supermodel Loopabella Van Squee.

'Lemme introduce you,' said Running Dave. 'This is Sigismond Electrique, from SPLANG FM.'

'What,' said Buddy, 'is SPLANG FM?'

'Radio Station,' said Running Dave. 'Fabulous fabulous. Our profile.'

Buddy nodded. Lou nodded. Both of them wondered what Running Dave was talking about.

'We're doing some interviews,' said Sigismond, a

small, spotty person with a grade two and horn-rimmed glasses. 'Plus a live taster for our listeners.'

'Are there a lot of them?'

'The Sigismond Electrique Bzzing Hour,' said Sigismond Electrique rather smugly, 'has an audience of one point five million in Smoke City alone. Plus planetary syndication, which means that everyone in the world hears it.'

'Ouch,' said Buddy, for the snuffbox had leaped in his pocket.

'So the guys better play well,' said Running Dave. 'Ha ha.'

'Ha ha,' said Buddy and Lou, in voices nearly as hollow as the Ghost's.

'You know where you are with Eric,' said Sigismond. 'No surprises.'

'Mnmyah,' said Buddy.

'I like that. None of your, like, here's some Camel Drumming we brought back from our holidays in like Oilystan. What we want is a lot of new stuff just like the old stuff. Only not the old stuff because we are really bored by the old stuff. Is it good, the new stuff?'

'Wait for it,' said Lou, trying to hide her nervousness by imagining what the Brothers Grime would have said about now.

'Bring it on,' said Sigismond, leaning back in his chair and allowing someone to fill his glass.

Lou dragged Buddy into a quiet corner. 'What are we going to *do*?' she said.

'Plan A,' said Buddy.

He pulled the snuffbox out of his pocket and laid it on the table. Beads of frost had formed on the outside, and it seemed to be pulsing to a hefty metal groove of its own.

'Keen,' said Lou.

'Very.'

'And the band have been practising "Bad Skoool".'

The snuffbox leaped nearly a metre in the air and came down spinning.

'I think Vlad's lads would like to be top of the bill,' said Lou.

'Go on stage last, you mean?'

'If there is still a stage to go on to.'

'Heh, heh,' said Buddy.

'Heh, heh is right.'

By eleven o'clock it was standing room only in the El Blotto Tea Rooms. Dense clouds of smoke eddied over the heads of the throng. The stage was dark and silent. The sound system was playing traditional Death Eric bagpipe music as a tribute to Kenyatta's tam-o'-shanter.

'Where are they?' said a woman in an elegant dress.

'Have you never been to a gig before?' said her boyfriend, who was wearing a business suit but had skull rings on most of his fingers.

'Of course, darling. The Smoke City School Choir Festival.'

'Bit different,' said the boyfriend. 'In rock and roll, people are late.'

'Late?'

'*Well* late. The bigger the band, the later they are – wait!'

A figure was moving on the stage: a roadie. The roadie stood on tiptoe and turned on the amplifiers. He wandered over to the drum kit and fiddled with something. ('Making sure Kenyatta's frying gear is all there,' said the man with the skull rings.) Then he took out a small lawnmower and pushed it over the area of stage in front of the bass amp. ('Fingers Trubshaw has to stand on turf,' said the skull-rings man.) Finally, he hung a small cage from a curly wire stand at the other side of the stage. ('Eric's bats,' said the skull-rings man. 'Ugh,' said the girl-friend, 'not only late, but disgusting.' 'Yes,' said the man, 'and sometimes he bites them.' 'Ugh and double ugh,' said the girlfriend, 'I am going home.' She started to push her way through the crowd towards the exit. The skull-rings man turned to follow her. Then he thought: roughly half the world are women, but there are only three of Death Eric, and he had a good place, right at the front, and he was not giving it up for anybody. So he stayed.)

The roadie shuffled off the stage. Green smoke began to billow from behind the speakers. The crowd roared like surf on a rocky shore. Inside the smoke, a heavy pulse of drums began. The crowd roared louder. On top of the drums there came a great walloping of bass. The smoke began to clear, revealing Fingers and Kenyatta playing in the shadows. A single white spotlight lanced out of the control box and settled on Rabid Dingo, crouching on a stand in front of a six-cab guitar stack. The vibrations of the bass set the guitar strings going. They began to throb and howl and feedback. Into the light shuffled a figure with long purple hair, a singlet, heavy tattoos and trousers just on the edge of falling down. The crowd threw

Smarties and bats. Eric (for the figure was of course him) strapped on the guitar without stopping the sobbing wail of feedback. He looked around him like a man not sure whether he was asleep or awake. His eye seemed to be caught by the red neon light of the pedal which lay on the stage flashing at him to STAMP HERE. He leaped two metres into the air. He came down like a thunderbolt. The feedback stopped. The huge, chunky beginning riffs of 'Chainsaw' thundered into the room.

The crowd stopped sounding like surf on a rocky shore and started sounding like a dam bursting. Heads were banging, bodies were popping and champagne corks were popping right back. The lads howled through 'Chainsaw', roared into 'Where's the Festival?' and out the other side, and thundered through a twenty-minute version of 'We Are Really Really Lost'. There were big foolish grins on the faces of one and all. Lou began to relax. Her father had bitten into his first bat, and showed every sign of having an excellent appetite for several more. Who needed a New Look? Everything was going to be –

Buddy's elbow drove into her ribs. 'WHA!' she

bellowed soundlessly (and actually rather crossly, for it had hurt).

'LOOK AT RUNNING DAVE!' roared Buddy, soundlessly as well of course, for children in feedback metal families must learn to lipread or starve. 'AND SIGISMOND WOSSNAME.'

Lou looked.

The Exec table was hopping and bopping. One of the suits was drumming on the table with two enormous cigars, and a stout lady was doing a flamenco dance among the glasses in the middle. But Running Dave was slumped in his chair sending a text on his phone. And Loopabella van Squee was checking her eye make-up with a small mirror. And Sigismond Electrique was filing his nails. All of them were the picture of boredom. While Lou watched, Running Dave raised his hand. At first she thought he was going to wave it enthusiastically above his head. Then she saw that he was . . .

'He's yawning!' cried Buddy.

Lou took a deep breath. She landed alongside Loopabella van Squee. During a quiet bit she said, 'Gosh, you're beautiful.'

Loopabella looked down through her long, long eyelashes. She saw a bright little girl, neatly dressed.

'Coooool,' she said, like a pigeon, and smiled with her beautiful bright-red lips.

'Aren't the band *great*?' said Lou.

'Yeah,' said Loopabella, not very enthusiastically.

'You don't think so?'

Loopabella had definitely heard of thinking, but she had never actually done much of it.

'I've heard them before,' she said. 'Doing this exact stuff. I thought they had a New Look.' She shrugged. 'Too bad.'

There was a sort of purring noise next to Lou. She looked up and saw Vlad, bending over so he could get a closer look at the beautiful Miss van Squee.

'Soon,' he said, 'vill show you New Look of Death Eric. Whirl Music.' He showed her his handsome profile. 'Is excellent, much better than this.'

The band suddenly came back in with a thunderous crash. Lou saw that Buddy was holding in his hand the snuffbox, which was now vibrating so hard it looked blurred. On the El Blotto Tea Rooms wall, the hands of the clock stood at ten seconds to midnight.

Buddy opened the snuffbox.

Somewhere in the room, a great bell tolled the hour.

All hell broke loose.

A long streak of greenish light whizzed out of the snuffbox, performed a corkscrew with triple axel, and . . . *changed*.

Eric was playing the 'Pig Train' Section Two riff, left hand miles up the neck, wringing mighty sobs and howls from Rabid Dingo. He headed for the mike, shaking his head, as if he had dimly noticed that something had happened to the mood of the audience.

This is not surprising.

Because what the audience was seeing was as follows:

The green corkscrew had twirled itself three times round Fingers Trubshaw's mike stand. It had then turned into an electric blue fog. The fog grew arms and legs. By the time the great bell had stopped tolling, Fingers Trubshaw's mike stand was occupied by a two-metre-tall skeleton, flashing in colours that ranged from lime green to sky blue, with a mop of bright-red hair on its head and lizardskin cowboy boots on its feet. The skeleton cocked what would have been an ear if skulls had ears, banged a boot on the ground, waited for Eric Thrashmettle to start singing and joined in with the chorus of 'Pig Train'.

The 'Pig Train' chorus in Section Two is one of those choruses that goes on for just about ever, with the Mormon Tabernacle Choir joining in and fly-pasts by the Red Arrows or other national aerobatic display team where available. The El Blotto gig was stripped down to bare essentials, so it should have been just Eric and Fingers singing. But Fingers could not get near his mike because of (a) stark terror and (b) the Ghost was already singing 'Bad Skoool' into it, and the band had changed the 'Pig Train' chords into the 'Bad Skoool' chords and were giving it everything they had. The undead have many voices, and the Ghost was singing in all of them at once. The effect was like a medium-range jetliner flying at tabletop height through quite a small nightclub. The engineers from SPLANG FM clutched their heads and dribbled, green fog leaking from their headphones. The crowd went mad.

'Bad Skoool' segued into the 'Pig Train' final solo, once compared by the chief reviewer of *SPLONG* magazine to 'a starship landing on a square mile of greenhouses'. The Ghost was a good enough musician to know it was time to stop singing, but (Buddy thought) he was enough of a show-off to be rather sad about it. If he had had a lower lip (thought Lou) it would have been sticking out like a church doorstep. Poor Ghost, thought Buddy, who was not without feelings. Poor Gh–, thought Lou.

She did not finish the thought, partly because she did not have time and partly because she had changed her mind. For the Ghost was not finished yet.

The enormous green skeleton raised one leg until the knee was level with its nose. Then it took the leg off, and held it in one hand. It pulled its skull off with the other hand, tossed it in the air and smacked it with the leg. The skull shot across the room, shrieking in an amused manner, whizzed back with a whirring noise, settled on the neck, tried looking backwards and forwards, then settled on sideways. Serpents coiled out of its ribcage, laughing heartily. Then the skeleton began to soften and melt, collapsing into a pile on the stage.

'Snuffbox!' hissed Lou. 'Or it'll make that –'

The pile grew smaller. What it lacked in size it made up for in stench.

'– smell,' said Lou.

'Too late,' said Buddy, snapping the snuffbox open. The pile of bad stuff on the floor flickered and wavered. A tendril of it snaked through the air and into the box. The rest of it followed. There was a small, distant cry of 'BAD SKOOOOL'. The the box lid slammed shut, and the Ghost was gone.

But the smell was still there. It was a truly awful smell, a mixture of lavatories and rubbish dumps and freezers with the power off and other things so frightful it was impossible to think of them for long enough to give them a name. The last great power chord of 'Pig Train' roared out into the club. 'Hangyou hangyou,' said Eric. The crowd stayed jammed together, tears streaming down its greenish faces.

A small man in a crash helmet and a gas mask bounded on to the stage. 'In the name of Health Safety Fire and Extra Safety Rules I hereby declare this, er, popular music performance a health hazard and against the law, plus it stinks,' he cried. 'Party's over. Ain't you got homes to go to? The emergency exits are open, please leave in an orderly manner.'

The crowd shook its heads, coughing and wheezing in the stench. It shuffled out into the street.

Vlad came sprinting round the front from the dressing room.

'But vot about Whirl Music?' he cried. 'Is time for excellent ood and –'

'Be quiet,' said Buddy.

This so astonished Vlad that he shut up.

Buddy was looking at Running Dave and Loopabella Van Squee. Their eyes were wide open. Their jaws hung down.

'Listen,' said Vlad. 'We are soooo sorry. I don't know what happened. Heads vill roll –'

'Roll?' said Running Dave, like a man surfacing from a deep trance. 'It went right across the room.'

'And back!' said Loopabella. 'Gross!'

'So *New*!' said Running Dave.

'Such a *look*!' said Loopabella.

'We *loved* it!' they both said together. 'It *rocked*! I mean it was practically *supernatural*!'

'Heh heh,' said Buddy weakly.

'I guess they were going to get into more new stuff next,' said Running Dave. 'Too bad they got closed down. But what a look! What a story! Live on radio, too! Can't wait for the new album!'

'Me too,' said Lou.

'Cool!' cried Running Dave. 'Champagne?'

'Bit early for us,' said Buddy and Lou.

*

It was late when they got back to Castle Bones, and they were tired. Next morning they were up bright and early at noon sharp. In the kitchen, Cookie was shuffling blearily to and fro. He made them a small breakfast of ham, eggs, fried potatoes, waffles, toast, syrup, marmalade and a double double papaya smoothie.

'Dunno what's got into everyone,' he said. 'Vlad, face like a boot. Honganians, right off their pies. Enid –'

'What about me?' said Enid. She was standing in the doorway, huge and beautiful.

'– would prob'ly like roughly what you had for breakfast but about twice the quantity,' said Cookie, going red. 'Heh heh. Three eggs or four?'

'I shall have a rice cake and a glass of fizzy water,' said Enid. 'Fizzy water is less fattening. Because of the bubbles.'

'Wha,' said Buddy and Lou.

'Vlad does not like big girls,' said Enid. Behind her, Cookie was tapping his forehead with his finger. 'Inside every big girl there is a small girl trying to get out.'

'Well you've got her pretty well trapped,' said Buddy.

'*Buddy!*'

'Yes, I must find my inner skinny person,' said Enid, apparently not hearing. 'Now I will take Vlad up a cup of tea. He was so disappointed not to play last night.'

'Enid,' said Buddy, 'there is an album to make, and it is not going to be a Whirl Music album.'

'Maybe,' said Enid, blowing lovingly on Vlad's tea as she drifted away. 'Maybe not.'

'Rrr,' said Lou. 'That *man!*'

'We've got to get rid of him, but the Ghost doesn't seem to scare him,' said Buddy. 'Something will turn up.'

'No it won't,' said Sid the Soothsayer, sticking his head round the door.

There was a shuffle of feet in the Hall of Columns, followed by a scream of terror. 'Sounds like the postman,' said Buddy.

In the hall, a big brown paper parcel was leaning against a column. The label said: *Anyone in the Death Eric entourage – For the Long Long Gallery, Castle Bones.*

'Oo,' said Lou. 'A lovely surprise, perhaps.' She had done very little shopping lately and was eager to unpack something. So she untied the rather primitive string that bound the parcel, and unwrapped the very old-fashioned brown paper and sacking with which it was swathed. A musty smell filled the air. A gilt frame, heavily carved, caught the light from the little round windows in the dome.

'Who is it?' said Buddy.

Lou manoeuvred the heavy picture into a beam of light. It was a portrait, painted in the slightly pop-eyed style of three hundred years ago. The subject was a woman with a pale face, black hair and red lips. The lips were parted, showing sharp white teeth.

'Gothalinda!' said Lou. 'She said she'd send one for the Long Long Gallery! Isn't it lovely!'

'If you like that sort of thing,' said Buddy, thinking, Give me a picture of a train or a bear any day.

'The roadies can take it up to the Long Long Gallery later,' said Lou. 'Let's get into the library.'

Into the library they went. Buddy laid the snuffbox on the table. Sun streamed in through the great stained-glass window. Buddy lifted the lid.

A few motes of dust drifted into the warm, bright air. They clumped up and grew. But not into a vast green skeleton or a stinking blob or any of the Ghost's show-offy forms. They merely became a weary shadow that drifted off to join the other shadows in the corners of the library's bookcases.

'What's the time?' said the Ghost's voice, dry and whispery as the wind in dead leaves.

'Quarter to two,' said Lou. 'You sound tired. Did you overdo it last night?'

'I thought I sang rather marvellously,' said the Ghost. 'I'm not as young as I was, is all.'

'Ah.'

'And now,' said the Ghost, 'I'll be getting along. Got cauldron water to turn to blood.' There was a sigh like wind in naked branches. 'Drudge, drudge,' said the Ghost, and was gone.

'Poor thing,' said Lou.

Buddy was looking at the portrait in the window, lizardskin boots, burst-sofa hair and all.

'Quite,' he said.

Lou followed her brother's eyes. 'And seeing yourself dressed like that and not being able to change it – what's wrong?'

For her brother had stood up. He had walked over to the window. He was staring with laser intensity at the disc of *Red Meat Pomeroy* in the stained-glass rocker's hand. He said, 'There's writing on it.'

'Wha,' said Lou, checking. There was, spidery

writing, round the disc's label. Old writing. Arabic, perhaps . . .

'It's written backwards,' said Buddy.

'Yes, dear,' said Lou. *What* was he on about now?

'Quick,' said Buddy. 'Come with me.'

Gripping his sister by the sleeve of her wine-red blazer, he towed her out of the room. They crossed the Hall of Columns, where Vlad was standing in the shadows near Gothalinda's picture, apparently deep in thought. They went up to Buddy's room. He took down a copy of L. P. Rekord's *Album Collector's Companion* and started to leaf through the pages.

'What are you *doing*?' said Lou, consumed with impatience.

'Peace, sister,' said Buddy, licking his thumb and leafing. 'Page two thousand four hundred and sixteen, two thousand four hundred and seventeen. Yep. Here. I'll read it to you. "Messages from Beyond the Grave. MFBG are usually found on the playout area" – that's the smooth bit next to the label on a vinyl record. "It is not known how they get there, but it would be foolish to discount the possibility that they are the work of Supernatural Engineers."'

'Wow,' said Lou, suddenly all ears.

'And listen to this,' said Buddy. '"*Messages from Beyond the Grave may be recorded forwards or backwards.*"'

'And the writing on the stained-glass window was backwards!' Lou frowned. 'But we played the record.'

Buddy took the *Red Meat Pomeroy* disc out of its sleeve. He wiped it with a hare's-fur cloth, gave it a light misting of isopropyl alcohol, and laid it reverently on the turntable. He swung the stylus arm in to the edge of the label. He dropped the stylus arm on the motionless record. Then, using the deejay skills of one born with headphones on his head, he revolved the disc in an anti-clockwise direction.

A voice spoke: a rumbling voice, with echoes, as if from the bottom of a deep, deep pit. *Listen, Ghost of Dave*, said the voice,

When the Transformer Lake like boils and boils and boils
When the raven flies above you
And a quarter million people cry 'We love you'
Until they're out of breath
And you take death
From another man

Then you can rest.
Yeah.

'Again,' said Lou. 'While I write it down.'

Buddy played it again. Lou wrote it down.

'Not much of a lyric,' said Lou.

'Total sixties rubbish, plus it doesn't scan,' said Buddy absently. 'Or rhyme properly. But it sounds like a bit of a problem. Getting lakes to boil. It's like saying you'll do something when hell freezes, i.e. never.'

'And getting two hundred and fifty thousand people to say they love him. I mean, he's quite a nice ghost as ghosts go. But not exactly lovable.'

'No.' Buddy looked at his shoes, which were Gucci. 'But of course,' he said, 'whoever said freezing hell was impossible didn't have access to roadies.'

'Roadies,' said Lou, 'can make anything happen.'

'Except maybe when they're in love with creeps.'

'Once a roadie, always a roadie,' said Lou. 'Let's go and see Enid.'

They walked down the Long Long Gallery and into the Hall of Columns. The portrait had not yet been moved. Vlad was still standing in front of it. He looked up as the children came past.

'Who is this voman?' he said.

'Countess Gothalinda Bathory,' said Lou. 'Why?'

'No reason,' said Vlad, almost dreamily. Then, remembering himself, 'No reason that is your business, anyvay.'

'Ah. Where's Enid?'

'Somevere,' said Vlad. 'Probably.'

They went into the kitchen. Flatpick the budgie was hooting gloomily. Cookie was complaining about the cauldron, whose water had mysteriously turned into Alka-Seltzer and foamed up the castle's already shaky drains. He dished out delicious mushroom omelettes with granary bread and salad. The band and some roadies drifted in.

'Not pies,' said Eric. 'Good.'

'Normally that Vlad comes in and forces me to make them,' said Cookie. 'But he's been in front of that picture all day so I thought, well, why not get a bit creative, like?'

'Picture,' said Enid, sipping a glass of fizzy water. Her eyes looked hollow, her powerful cheeks wasted.

Even Sid the Soothsayer noticed. 'Peaky?' he said. 'You'll be better soon.'

Enid buried her face in her hands.

Buddy finished his lunch and went to sit next to her. 'I've got a list of things to do,' he said. 'Would you mind helping?'

Enid raised her face from her hands. Her eyes were wild, her face like a rugged landscape lashed by thunderstorms.

'Leave me alone,' she said.

Buddy's mouth fell open. This was Enid, the most helpful, the kindest, the best . . . well, when you had a father like Eric and mother like Wave and a main roadie like Enid, it was obviously going to be Enid who was your guide, adviser and friend, Vlad or no Vlad.

'C'mon,' said Lou, pulling him away from the table. Buddy allowed himself to be led, like a boy in a dream. Once they were safely in the library, Lou turned on him. 'How can you be such an *idiot*?' she hissed.

Buddy shook his head to get rid of the feeling that he had just stopped a Number 30 bus with his left ear.

'Wha,' he said.

'It's sooo obvious. Vlad is out there gooping at a portrait of Gothalinda, so is it any wonder Enid is really upset?'

'Upset wha.'

'*Honestly!*' said Lou, stamping a nicely polished court shoe. 'Are you *blind*! She's *heartbroken*! Poor *Enid*! What are we going to *do*?'

'Do?' said Buddy. 'You mean Enid fancies Vlad so she won't tell the Honganians to go away and Vlad fancies Gothalinda so Enid's fed up and nothing's happening and they're not going to get the album out in time and we're going to be miserable forever and have to eat those ghastly pies and we need a scheme to fix this? It's obvious. We invite Gothalinda to her old home for a bit. She will be missing it by now.'

'Gosh,' said Lou, slightly taken aback by the awesome power of her brother's mind. 'Brilliant.'

'And now,' said Buddy when they had written to Gothalinda, 'let us go and play some music.'

They sat in the Gothic cottage. The music transported them on airy mathematical wings through the canopy of yew branches and into the night, where they cruised the eddies of the air with the bats and owls.

It is a lovely thing when you have wanted something to turn up, and something does turn up, and life becomes clear.

Clear?

Clear to Buddy and Lou. Perhaps not to you, reader.

Wait for it.

7

It was always hard to work out what was going on in Eric's head. But that night in the studio there was a new atmosphere. He strapped his guitar on the right way round, for one thing. He turned the amp from STANDBY to ON himself without help. And when he went to the lavatory he did not fall down it.

'I wonder if he's ill?' said Lou to Enid. 'Enid?'

But Enid just shrugged and wandered off.

There did not seem to be any Honganians about.

Eric walked into a corner and started playing a small but savage riff. Kenyatta picked it up. Fingers thumped in there like a big woolly sledgehammer. And after a few false starts there was a kind of a tune, with a verse, another verse and a bridge, which is the bit of singing in the middle that is not a verse. And Eric was using a pen – *the right end* of a pen – to write some words on the back of an old guitar-string envelope.

'Stone me,' said Buddy. 'He's writing a song.'

'Wanna do a demo,' said Eric to the microphone. 'Called er "Doom Lagoon". Take, er, three –'

'One,' said the engineer.

'– whatever. A-ONE, two.'

And off went Death Eric into a brand-new song.

The children tiptoed out. 'Great!' they said.

'Vot's great?' snapped a voice. And there was Vlad, his cloak spread like bat's wings in the gloom.

Lou did actually find him rather alarming. So actually did Buddy. But both of them had just been listening to Death Eric on top form, and this tended to give you a lot of confidence as well as a slight ringing in the ears.

'Dad playing with his band,' said Lou defiantly.

'Without all that Honganian rubbish,' said Buddy with awful frankness.

There was a moment of silence. Vlad's eyes narrowed, and unless Buddy was gravely mistaken they glowed with a reddish fire.

'Children,' he purred in a voice like a reptile cat's, 'it ees past your bedtime.' Then he brushed past them in a waft of chilly air.

No matter how alarming you are, it is not tactful to tell children it is past their bedtime. It is still less tactful if you are a semi-vampire who is trying to suck up the energy of the world's leading feedback metal band by using Love Hypnotism on its main roadie.

So Buddy and Lou leaned against the back of a carved column, and watched Vlad open the studio door and put his head in, and heard the music stop, and Vlad say, 'Ah! Soon I will send in marvellous Honganian musicians!'

Then they heard Eric's voice say, 'Not really.'

'But Honganian Whirl Music is the New –'

'I'm, er,' said Eric's voice, 'writing an, er. Later, man. Shut the door after you.'

There was a huge electric crash as he dropped his guitar. Still, it had been an impressive speech.

'Vot?' said Vlad, apparently shocked, staring at the closed door.

'I've never heard him like that before,' said Buddy.

'Something's getting on his nerves,' said Lou.

'Or someone. Eh, Vlad?'

'Still,' said Lou, 'I expect Enid will sort it out. She's in control round here.'

Vlad made a noise like one of Lou's pet snakes, and swirled himself off down the corridor.

'Hah!' said Buddy.

'Excellent,' said Lou. 'They'll be writing songs all night. They can start recording tomorrow. And if they're recording, the roadies won't have anything to do, so we can get ready to fix the stuff in the rhyme and deal with that Ghost.'

'What,' said Buddy, 'can stand in our way?'

All night, Fingers' bass knocked dust and earthworms from between the paving stones in the Hall of Columns. In the morning, the children collided with Enid.

'Well?' they said.

'Well what?' said Enid.

'Well, how many songs did Dad write last night?'

'One,' said Enid.

There were black circles under her eyes, and her face looked like a rugged landscape feeling the first cold breath of winter.

'Is that all?' said Buddy.

'He can write five a night when he gets going,' said Lou.

'That,' said Enid, 'is when the studio is not full of Honganians eating heavy pies and playing the ood out of time and the zither out of tune.'

'They got in?' said Buddy. 'How?'

Enid hung her head. 'I let them in,' she said. 'I know, I know. But Vlad was nice to me and everything went black. I hate myself for it.'

Even Lou felt her patience with Enid stretched rather thin. Obviously it was time to distract her.

'Look at this.' She passed the paper with the words of the Ghost's spell across to Enid. 'Would it take long to organize?'

Enid frowned at the paper, her huge but beautiful lips moving slightly. 'Make a lake boil?' she said. 'Make two hundred and fifty thousand people tell a two-metre greenish skeleton what stinks like a ruptured sewage pipe that they love him? Easy.'

'Oh, good,' said Buddy.

'I was joking,' said Enid. 'Only it was hard to tell because it wasn't funny.'

'Yes,' said Buddy, who was a bit alarmed by this new, desperate Enid.

'Where's Vlad?' said Lou, rather more subtly.

Enid turned on her a face like a huge and rugged landscape under which lay the epicentre of a medium-sized earthquake.

'In the Long Long Gallery,' she said. 'Sitting in a chair. In front of the portrait of Gothalinda. Beside which he has lit a black candle. And at which he is like gazing. With dog-like devotion. Werewolf-like,' said Enid, correcting herself.

'Oh,' said Lou.

'Men!' said Enid.

Shoving herself to her feet, she strode out of the room.

'You know what?' said Lou. 'I hope Gothalinda gets that letter soon.'

The children finished their breakfast in silence, then went to practise peaceful music.

A great stillness hung over Castle Bones. Stillness, but not peace. All right, peace. But the sort of peace you get when you have jumped out of an aeroplane and are floating on your parachute towards a cold and shark-infested sea.

There is a word for that kind of peace. The word is 'temporary'.

The music finished. The children put their instruments down. Buddy seemed to be thinking.

'I've got an idea,' he said finally. 'It's in the *Tales*.'

'Of the Brothers Grime?' said Lou, touching the book.

'Yeah. You told me. It was about the Invention of Lunch.'

'Ah,' said Lou. 'You mean when the wise man Fong, noticing three ants sharing a crumb, suddenly realized that humans could do the same thing, only on a larger scale?'

'Exactly,' said Buddy.

'But we've *had* lunch,' said Lou.

'Not lunch,' said Buddy. 'Festivals.'

'Wha?' said Lou.

'Let's go for a walk,' said Buddy.

'Walk?'

'C'mon.'

First, they went and stood on the edge of the Transformer Lake.

'Note the bowl-shaped sides, ideal for sitting on,' said Buddy. 'And the small flat island ideal for a stage with a band on.'

Lou turned and gaped at him. She saw his exact point.

'Onward,' said Buddy, and led her to the Gothic cottage on its hill. 'Note the small terrace, ideal for the refreshment of the ears of people blasted by metal.'

Lou's eyebrows clattered against her hairline. She got his precise drift.

They visited the Hall of Columns, which would make a perfect bar. They wandered among the glowing bulbs casting ghastly shadows in the Valve Crypt, which would certainly make an excellent chill-out room (though rather a hot one). And they saw with new eyes the Library, the Long Long Gallery, the Real Tennis Courts, the Rifle Range, the Jousting Lists and the Observatory.

'Well?' said Buddy.

'Perfect,' said Lou.

'Ladees and gemmen,' said Buddy. 'Death Eric Productions proudly presents . . .'

'Death Eric at Home in the Castle Bones Late Summer Festival!'

'Tickets strictly limited to a quarter of a million!'

'Guest artistes!'

'*Ghost* artistes! Death Eric Live at –'

'*Undead* at –'

'– *undead* at Castle Bones!'

'The record company will *love* it!'

'*Just* what they want!'

They looked at each other in a great amaze.

'Cosmique!' cried Buddy.

'Phat!' cried Lou. 'New Look, New Album!'

Then they went and had a working tea with lashings of pop.

'Right,' said Buddy after half an hour's hard labour. 'I've got an agenda.'

'A what?'

'A list of stuff that needs doing. Number one, publicity.'

'We'll get the publicists to do it. No problem.'

'Good. Number two, technical. Sound on the island, lights everywhere, portable studio for recording album.'

'Which is what roadies are for. No problem.'

'Good. Number three, the Ghost. World fame, lake boiling, crowd singing, all that, as specified.'

'Roadies again. And Dad to lead the singing.'

'Number four, ticket sales. Two hundred phones, right?'

'Right.'

'Good. Number five, the music.'

'Which is Dad and the lads plus support. Er . . .'

'Quite. If we don't get rid of the Honganians people will throw things.'

'Quarter of a *million* people.'

'And Running Dave will not be impressed.'

'Hmm. Perhaps if we were to talk to Enid . . .'

The kitchen door opened. Heavy boots crunched on discarded chicken bones, and the hem of a huge print dress whistled around tattooed knees.

'Hello, children!' cried Enid.

Buddy eyed her with grave suspicion. She looked unnaturally pink, and her eyes were glittering.

'What's wrong with you?' he said.

Lou kicked him savagely under the table.

'So you are happy, dear Enid!' she said.

'He looked at me again. With his eyes. I love him I love him I love him,' said poor deluded Enid.

'Got it,' said Buddy, feeling he might vomit.

'Meanwhile,' said Lou, seizing the moment, 'we've got a festival to organize!'

'Brilliant idea!' cried Enid. 'Bring it on!'

Lou and Buddy brought it on. Lists were made. Organization commenced.

First and most important, Enid put on her newest print dress, polished her tattoos to a high shine and barged into Sigismond Electrique's studio, trashing receptionists and security men.

'We are having a festival,' she said, shaking off a part-time Sumo wrestler.

'I dunno,' said Sigismond Electrique, who was wearing headphones and scowling at a bit of paper bearing his listener figures in far Cathay. 'I got a billion listeners out there, will they be interested in a festival in lil' ol' Smoke City?'

'Certainly will,' said Enid. 'Shall we have lunch?'

'Oh all right,' said Sigismond Electrique. 'Where?'

'I am flying you to Scargoville,' said Enid.

'Cor,' said Sigismond, for Scargoville was the lunch capital of the world.

'The chopper is waiting,' said Enid, putting a foot forward so Sigismond could see her really lovely absolutely huge red shoes.

'Woof!' said Sigismond, hauling off his headphones.

*

'How did it go?' said Buddy to Enid, when she returned to Castle Bones later that afternoon.

'Fine,' said Enid. 'He's giving the festival masses of free publicity. They always do if you give them snails and champagne and threaten them a tiny bit. Her eyes fogged over. 'Where's Vlad?'

'In the Long Long Gallery,' said Buddy.

'By candlelight,' said Lou.

'Oh,' said Enid.

Her face fell like a huge rugged landscape experiencing landslides. She shuffled off.

Buddy turned on the radio. Sure enough, there was the voice of Sigismond Electrique, slightly fizzed up with champagne, saying, 'Go to Castle Bones next week! Everyone else is! Be at Bones or be alone!'

'She did a great job,' said Buddy.

'Sure did,' said Lou. 'Listen to those phones ring on the ticket desk.'

'Continuous,' said Buddy, raising his voice to make himself heard over the racket of equipment lorries arriving.

'Phase one begun,' said Lou.

All that week the phones rang and the lorries rolled in. On the second day, a small red van zigzagged among the mighty artics, and a postman climbed out, looked nervously about him and sprinted to the front door.

Buddy and Lou were waiting for him. He handed over the letters, gave a quick, nervous smile and took off up the drive like a maniac.

'Here it is,' said Lou.

She was holding a black-edged envelope of thick cream paper. The address was written in brownish-red ink; at least, Buddy hoped it was ink. The stamp showed a double-headed eagle, apparently printed with a potato.

'Open it!' cried Buddy.

Lou said, 'All *right*,' because actually quite a lot depended on what was inside the envelope, and she was nervous. She tore the flap.

The letter was two sheets, bearing big writing in more of the brownish-red (hopefully) ink, though there were several small flies stuck in it, so it seemed likely that it might be –

'What does it *say*?' said Buddy.

'Ah. Yes. "Dear Childrens. Yes it is indeed possible that I can come see vunce again my dear Castle Bones. But my Counsellor in Blood Group says I have got to get a life. Of my own, I mean. I have finished Revamp, though, and I am feeling strong. I vill try very hard to come – because I love darkness and I am still a sucker for childrens but since Revamp not in the old vay! Expect me ven you see me.

your cool friend

Gothalinda.

P.Sss. You say you have got a person called Vlad there from Hongania. Is this the Vlad that they call the Inhaler who has got quite a big castle in Transylvania? If so he is fantastic –" end of page,' said Lou, 'next page, hang on, yes, "he is fantastic show-off, thoroughly unreliable and I strongly suspect he is part-time wampyr in denial. Votch him. Your loving friend G." Certainly sounds like our Vlad.'

'So maybe she's coming and maybe she isn't,' said Buddy. 'What do we do now?'

'Carry on,' said Lou. 'And I think that Vlad would enjoy seeing at least part of the letter. And Enid wouldn't. So we'll show it to both of them.'

'But it says he's a creep.'

'Part of it does,' said Lou, smiling sweetly. 'Part of it says the opposite.'

Her brother gazed at her with dawning admiration. 'I see what you *mean*!' he said.

'Off we go,' said Lou, briskly. 'The Long Long Gallery, I think.'

Up to the Long Long Gallery they went. Halfway along was a glow of candlelight and a cloud of cigarette smoke, and Vlad in a carved chair, his chin on his hand, his awful black eyes brooding on the portrait of Gothalinda.

'Hi, Vlad!' cried Buddy and Lou. 'We've got some great news for you!'

Vlad's eyes stayed on the picture. 'Like you have maybe got a fatal illness?'

'Ha, ha,' cried Lou gaily, though shocked.

'Quite the reverse!' cried Buddy.

'We've got a letter from a friend of ours,' said Lou.

'Oh look!' said Buddy, faking surprise. 'What a coincidence! The one in the picture you're looking at!'

Vlad's head came round so fast his neck clicked.

'Wha,' he said.

'Gothalinda. She's really cool!'

'Ya. Wha?'

'And she *knows* you!'

'She does?' said Vlad.

One of his eyes was looking at Buddy, the other

at Lou. The children moved apart to see what would happen. The eyes followed them.

'Look!' cried Lou, thrusting the letter into his hand.

Vlad read it. At first he looked bored, as selfish people do when they are reading something that is not about them. But as he came to the P.Sss. his eyes bulged, and he read it again. And again. Then he kissed the paper. Then he licked his lips in a way that made Buddy think that the reddish-brown ink might indeed be something that was not actually ink, unless Vlad was an ink drinker, which seemed unlikely.

'Er, Vlad,' said Lou, to the point as always, 'what's a wampyr?'

'Hmm,' said Vlad, his red tongue going round his lips. 'No idea.'

'It's a way of spelling vampire,' said Buddy.

'Oo,' said Lou. 'Anyway. Poor old Gotha's been in a clinic. On the Honganian border. Called Bad Tripp. If you hurry, you'll catch her there.'

'I know zis clinic,' said Vlad, hauling a mobile phone from his waistcoat pocket and battering buttons. 'I ring it now. Ja?' He started to talk in no known language. 'Ah.' He put away the telephone. 'She has left,' he said. 'Too bad.'

'Too bad,' said the children. 'So, what now?'

'I admire her portrait like knight of old admiring lady love,' said Vlad. 'Und then Honganians go to top the bill at the festival – that is, ve help Death Eric to top the bill.'

'Oh,' said the children, gloomy again. 'Fine.' They shuffled off to the Gothic cottage and played Streik's Music For Playing While Others Work. Down below, Castle Bones and its grounds fairly hummed with activity. Riggers rigged, sound engineers sounded off, lighting people lit –

Reader, we could trudge through the whole dismal list, but we will not. In telling a story, it is important to stick to the bits that are interesting, amusing, or help the action along. Telling you that the Plug Man changed three thousand four hundred and eleven tiny little thirteen-amp fuses is none of the above.

Interesting bits, then. Six days to go.

On Day 1, nobody told the band what was happening in case they got distracted from song-writing. Sid the Soothsayer sprained his ankle doing an anti-rain dance.

On Day 2, Eric had written eight songs and needed another two. The air in the studio was of low quality, being full of the smell of rock and rollers. Everyone was getting edgy when the door bounced open and Rick the Thick, stupidest of roadies, said to Enid, 'Where d'you want fish and chip vans, then?'

'La la la,' said Enid, very loud.

But Rick the Thick would not be daunted. 'Plus,' he said, 'the landscapers want to know, where do you want the extra landscapin' and lawns laid, and that?'

Fingers Trubshaw had headphones on, but it would take more than headphones to deafen him to what was closest to his heart. He tore them off his head.

'Lawns?' he said.

Kenyatta had been doing some lipreading of his own.

'Fish fryin'?' he said.

Fingers unstrapped his bass. Kenyatta put down his drumsticks.

'What exactly is going on here?' said Fingers.

'We needing to be told,' said Kenyatta.

'Cheese? Bats?' said Eric, who could not hear, did not know how to lipread, and was wondering what rhymed with 'chimney' in a rather complicated lyric he was writing for a track entitled 'Smokestacks of Hell'.

'Switch it off!' cried Fingers to the control room.

'All off!' cried Kenyatta. 'Now. Enid. Explain. What is this about fish vans?'

'And lawncare?'

'Ahaha,' said Enid nervously. 'We are having a bit of a festival, and we need food people and lawn people, and because the songs were going so well we didn't want . . . to . . . trouble you . . .'

'No trouble,' said Fingers grimly.

'None at all,' said Kenyatta sternly. 'If there is fish to be fried, it is me that is going to fry it.'

'And if there are lawns to be cared for, it is Green Fingers Trubshaw who will do the caring.'

'There are songs to write,' said Enid. 'A gig to plan.'

'Songs?' said Fingers. 'We've got plenty. We'll play, of course. But right now there's long grass out there.'

'Gig?' said Kenyatta. 'We've been practising solid for weeks. We'll play, natch. But just now I have other fish to fry.'

Both of them walked out of the studio.

'Wo,' said Eric, looking slightly worried. 'Walkout, right?'

'Ye-es,' said Enid. 'But you have got eight songs out of ten.'

'Actually nine,' said Lou, who had been watching the above with a sense of mounting horror. 'If you do a cover of "Bad Skoool" by Aluminium Dave Krang. As a special favour to us.'

'"Bad Skoool"?' Eric said. 'Good tune.' He began to hum. His fingers moved on the guitar, picking out the 'Bad Skoool' riff, but with a back-beat and twiddles, so Buddy felt a keen sweat break out on his brow, and Lou's feet wanted to boogie. 'Yep,' said Eric. '*Nice.*'

'*Nice,*' said a huge voice somewhere in the deeps of the castle.

'Wha,' said Eric. 'Who?'

'The ghost of Aluminium Dave Krang,' said Buddy.

On Day 3, Enid and Eric were crouched over a table modelled on the ones used to track bomber squadrons in the 1940s. Instead of small cardboard bombers, there were big metal rock bands. Various managers were clustered round. Buddy and Lou were watching.

'The opening act is Stormy Chipolata,' said Enid. 'Followed by Iron String. Followed by Magnesium Opus –'

'Nah,' said someone in leathers. 'No way are Opus playin' after String.'

'String,' said another person in what seemed to be a diving suit, 'are no way playing higher on the bill than Chipolata.'

'OK,' said Enid. 'Opus. Then String. Then Chipolata.'

'Whaaaa?' said a man in a sharkskin suit.

'Oo,' said Enid, suddenly going pink, for Vlad had glided in.

'Vot is all this noise?' said Vlad. 'Ah. I see. You are organizing running order.' He hovered over the table like an enormous bat. 'But I see no Honganian Folk Orchestra,' he said.

'Hongania?' said Sharkskin. 'What?'

'Whirl Music,' snarled Vlad. 'New Look, wave of the future. Did you not hear?'

'Nah,' said Sharkskin.

'Hello everyone!' cried a clear young voice. 'Telephone for Mr Vlad! Mr Vlad!' And Buddy trotted into the room. He and Lou had been listening on the sidelines, and it was now definitely time to act. Today, he was acting Stepin Fetchit, the Messenger Boy.

'Tell 'em I vill ring back,' said Vlad.

'No can do, sir,' said Buddy. 'Long distance, bad line, limited money for call box, the lady says.'

'Go away!' said Vlad, opening his sharp white teeth and hauling Sharkskin's neck towards them.

'Yes, sir!' cried Buddy. 'I'll tell the Countess you're neckin' with someone else, heh heh —'

'Countess?' said Vlad, dropping Sharkskin with a crash. 'Gimme the phone,' he roared, brushing into the control room and picking up the receiver. 'Yeah?' He turned his voice into a smooth purr. 'I mean, hello, Countess, what a pleasure, nay honourrr.'

'Hmm,' said a voice on the other end. There was an enormous crackling on the line. 'I long to see you. Vot are you vearing?'

'Vearing?' said Vlad. 'Oh, you know, cloak, suit, clean underwear. Daily.'

More crackling. The voice said something that sounded like, 'I should hope so too.'

'Pardon?' said Vlad.

More crackles. 'I hope your socks are blue,' said the voice.

'For you, I vill alvays vear blue socks.'

'Good,' said the voice.

'Have we already met?' said Vlad. 'Your voice

is familiar. You sound . . . well, marvellously young.'

Crackle, crackle, went the line –

All right. You will perhaps be thinking, this all happened at a very convenient moment, just as Vlad was about to suck out all of Sharkskin's blood and the festival was going to end before it had even started. Dodgy, you will be saying. Too much of a coincidence. Do me a favour, I was not born yesterday.

You are right, of course. The truth is this. Buddy and Lou had seen how things were going. The lady's voice on the phone was not actually Gothalinda's. It was Lou's. The crackling was Lou eating crisps as she talked, to simulate the sound of a very bad line –

– crackle, crunch, ulp. 'Seven hundred and twenty-two next birthday,' said Lou, crossing her fingers. 'Vich I hope to spend with you, this comink veekend.'

'Dollink,' breathed Vlad. 'Richest of darknesses. Love of my –'

'Beep, beep, beep,' said Lou, cunningly simulating a run-out-of-money noise before she was actually sick into the phone. 'Eeeeeee.'

Vlad slammed down the receiver. Sharkskin had left. Enid was gazing upon him with a dangerous glint in her eye.

'Who was that?' she said.

'Friend of a friend,' mumbled Vlad, surprised to find himself sweating, something undead people seldom do.

'Oh,' said Enid flatly.

'Gosh,' said Vlad, swallowing hard. The Love Hypnotism seemed not to be working. 'Is that the time already?'

He glided away, looking nervously over his shoulder.

On Day 4, Vlad seemed to have gone invisible. Buddy and Lou went to check through the Leper's Vent in the bedroom wall. The Honganian manager was sitting at his dressing table. The face in the mirror was semi-transparent, except where it was pale green.

'Fantastic!' said Buddy. 'He's got a really serious illness!'

Lou elbowed him aside. 'No such luck,' she said. 'That is an avocado face mask.'

'But the eyes!'

'Not eyes,' said Lou. 'Cucumber slices.'

'Wha.'

'To make himself lovely for Gothalinda,' said Lou.

'Silly fool,' said Buddy. 'Now, then. Let's go and talk to Enid.'

Reader, it would be an immense joy to explain in detail the exact conversation Buddy and Lou had with Enid. But some of it is too boring (see Days 1, 2 and 3). And some of it, particularly the special effects part, is still on the Top Secret list.

Oh, all right then. Just a little hint.

At 3 p.m., Eric wandered down to the Transformer Lake, climbed into the performers' barge, and was carried across to the island, on which now stood a splendid state-of-the-art music stage, based on a crashed starship.

Also on the barge was Fingers Trubshaw, wearing corduroy trousers stained deep green by intensive mowing, and Kenyatta McClatter, fingers still greasy from analysing the lard quality in the many chip vans scattered here and there in the grounds of Castle Bones.

They climbed off at the landing quay and walked up to the stage for a run-through, which is like a dress rehearsal, but musical. The new material seemed to go well; though the performers could not be seen, because of the heavy curtain drawn across the front of the stage.

Most of the way through the set, the band were heard to launch into the big, roaring riff that was the beginning of 'Bad Skoool'. Just as the voice was due to come in, the sound of screaming was heard onstage. Roadies burst out of the curtain and the sides and the back, hurled themselves into the Transformer Lake and started swimming as fast as they could towards the mainland. It was noted that the hair of Rick the Thick, which had been deep black and joined up with his eyebrows, was now snow white. When friends on the mainland asked them what they had seen, they said –

Enough. End of hint. There are now two mere days to go before the actual festival.

At which, dear reader, all these mysteries will be revealed.

And more besides.

'I can't *wait*!' said Lou eagerly.

'You'll just have to,' said Buddy. 'What's that ghastly noise?' He looked out of the window of the Gothic cottage, where he and Lou had been drinking a mug of refreshing Horlicks. 'Oops.'

The Thrashmettle children trained powerful binoculars on the stage.

They saw a rabble of Honganians. In front of the rabble stood Vlad, one arm out, cape flowing in the breeze in a classic rock-god pose. 'Now,' boomed his hugely amplified voice, 'vill be singing infectious Honganian song "Eat Nice Brussels Sprouts in Name of Revolution". You are all commanded to dance or else.'

The band started to play. Vlad started to sing. Flat.

Buddy looked at Lou. Lou looked at Buddy. Each knew what the other was thinking.

Vlad did not want to be a Manager, giving Eric a New Look. He wanted to be a Star.

Eek.

Day 5. Panic, naturally.

'What will happen will happen,' said Buddy, watching Fingers Trubshaw scream past the window on an out-of-control Lawnshava and carve a broad avenue through a stand of yew trees.

'How very true,' said Lou, ducking slightly as Kenyatta McClatter thundered past the other window in a blazing chip van. The chip van plunged into the Transformer Lake, leaving a huge lard slick, through which Kenyatta could be seen striking out for the shore.

'Zen's Distraction in Time of Travail, I think,' said Buddy.

'A-two, *three*,' said Lou.

And away went the Thrashmettle children into music land, where all was calm and serene.

At Castle Bones, nothing was calm, and few things serene. Enid's operations desk was covered in telephones, all ringing continuously.

'Perimeter guard. Gates still shut, but mass fence invasion.'

'Throw 'em out.'

'Ticket desk. We're running out.'

'Put the prices up.'

'Rusty Nayle say they want a twenty-five-pounder field gun and four Dobermann pinschers in their dressing room.'

'Give 'em a water pistol and a teddy bear.'

'All the lights on the right-hand side of the stage have been colonized by bats.'

'Let sleeping bats lie, sorry, hang.'

On it went. And on. At midnight the Ghost appeared and made tea for everyone. But nobody had time to drink it.

Day 6 dawned grey and rainy. The gates opened at 7 a.m. 250,000 ticket holders surged into the grounds with a roar.

The festival was on.

8

Buddy and Lou rose at nine, had power showers, put on their festival gear (exactly the same as their everyday gear, but with false beards in case they were recognized) and went for a walk. Castle Bones itself was ringed by huge security men. Outside the security men, paparazzi clambered around in trees and reporters from *WHO?* magazine interviewed everything that was breathing and quite a lot of things that were not.

''Scuse me,' said a reporter to Lou. 'You

wouldn't be Lulubelle Flower Fairy Thrashmettle, would you?'

'What a stupid name,' said Lou cunningly. 'Ask yourself, is this what a midget with a beard would be called?'

'Hmm,' said the reporter, who seemed none too bright. 'See what you mean. Pass, friend.'

'Thank you *so* much,' said Buddy with great sarcasm. And the two young folks mingled with the crowd.

It was some crowd. It swarmed in the yew woods, festooned the crags and washed its hair in the waterfalls. The air was greyish and dampish, but nobody noticed. For on the stage in the middle of the lake, metal music throbbed and crashed. Seated round the great bowl of land surrounding the water, the crowd headbanged and idiot danced, and every now and then someone crowd surfed down from the top to the edge of the water, then dived elegantly in to frenzied applause from all sides. The lawns were in perfect condition, and the appetizing whiff of fried fish drifted up the slopes like smoke up the crater of a volcano. A really splendid time was being had by all.

'I wonder where the Ghost is?' said Buddy.

'Here,' said a voice like someone at the bottom of a well; someone rather nervous, actually.

'Can't see you,' said Buddy.

'I'm embarrassed,' said the Ghost. 'I mean, look at the state of me.'

'Like I said, can't see you,' said Buddy.

'It must be awful,' said Lou. 'I mean, you're not really used to people, are you?'

'No,' said the Ghost. 'I mean, the grave is, well, a fine place if you like that sort of thing, but private. I haven't seen this many people for thirty-five years. I've got . . . well, stage fright.'

'Tell you what,' said Lou. 'You can do two-metre skeleton and stinking blob with or without fangs. Can't you do ordinary boring person in jeans and T-shirt? To get used to everyone?'

'Oh,' said the Ghost. 'Well. I suppose I could try.' There was a sort of shimmer in the air. The shimmer became a short fat man in a three-piece suit with flared trousers and huge lapels.

'There!' said Lou. 'Totally normal.' She caught Buddy's eye and frowned, before her brother could say, yeah, well, except for the light-blue skin, the talons and the empty eye sockets. 'Fancy an ice cream?'

208

'Yeah,' said the Ghost, still nervous. 'No. Dunno.'

'Go on,' said Lou.

'OK,' said the Ghost, with a shy yet totally terrifying light-blue grin.

'That's the spirit!' said Buddy.

They started towards the ice-cream van. The Ghost's mood improved enough for it to make scornful remarks about the lead guitarist of Uranium Hell, and his non-solid nature made it easy for him to get through the crowd. As they stood in the ice-cream van queue, he started to make sarcastic comments about people's piercings. It sounded to Lou as if he was getting his nerve back. They arrived at the front of the queue.

'What d'you want?' said Buddy.

'World fame. Eternal rest.'

'I mean flavour?'

'Oh. Something pale blue or green.'

Buddy got two chocolate chips and a pistachio surprise for the Ghost. They strolled off.

'Let's sit down and listen to the –'

'Ello ello ello,' said a voice behind them. When Lou looked round, she saw a large squashy man with a walkie-talkie clipped to his belt. Across his horribly tight-stretched T-shirt was written the word SECURITY. 'Wot's all this, then?' said the security man.

'Wot's all wot?' said Buddy, never one to suffer fools gladly, particularly squashy ones.

'Armbands,' said the security guard. 'Come on, let's see 'em.'

Lou pulled out her laminate and flashed it. Buddy pulled out his laminate and flashed it.

'Seems to be in order,' said the security man grudgingly. 'Wot about your nasty-looking fiend? I mean friend, ho, ho.'

'Ho, ho,' said Buddy, not laughing. 'He is with us. He lives here.'

'In a manner of speaking,' said Lou.

'I do not care if he is with the Queen of the Cannibal Islands herself in person,' said the security man. 'I wanna see an armband or laminate.'

'I told you,' said Buddy. 'He lives here.'

'Sort of,' said Lou again.

'You don't like me, do you?' said the Ghost, losing his hard-earned confidence.

'More'n my job's worth to comment, really,' said the security man. 'But since you ask, no.'

'Ah,' said the Ghost, in a voice like the creak of

a vault door. 'Now we get the truth. At last, an honest person.'

'No,' said Lou, feeling things were falling apart.

'ENOUGH,' roared the Ghost. Thunder rolled around the valley.

'Keep your voice down . . . aaAAIEE,' said the security man.

For the pale-blue person in the awful suit had suddenly started to grow. The suit exploded into little rags that wiggled off into the crowd. The vast blue man became a vast green blob that floated up in the air like a balloon. It swelled and swelled until it burst. An awful smell bounced away over the throng, mowing down all in its path. The security man stared with his jaw hanging open. A pistachio surprise cornet with two scoops plummeted out of the sky and into his mouth.

'GGG,' said the security man, cone sticking out between his lips, eyes bulging.

'Leave him,' said Buddy. 'Ghost?'

'He's been insulted in his own place,' said Lou. 'He won't come back.'

'But what about the gig?' said Buddy. 'What about world fame, eternal rest, all that?'

'He's an artist,' said Lou. 'Dead temperamental.'

'Dead, yes,' said Buddy. 'But temperamental? I –'

'Oh, shut up and eat your ice cream,' said Lou, showing that she was pretty nervous herself. 'It's time we were backstage.'

This was true. The support bands had finished. Onstage, the roadies were putting the final touches to Death Eric's gear. Backstage, all was quiet professionalism except for Eric, who was running round in circles making grabs at the air and saying, 'Norbert! Norbert!'

Enid came up with a bat cage and handed Eric one of the tiny winged mammals. 'Here you are,' she said. 'Use it wisely.'

'Yeah,' said Eric, hanging the bat on the inside of his cloak, where it remained contentedly. 'I shall call it Norbert Two. The first bat I shall call Norbert the Brave.'

'It's a free country,' said Enid. Her eyes shifted, and she went pink and glassy. 'Oh hello, Vlad.'

Onstage, a huge metal voice was addressing the crowd: 'LADEESN GEMMEN BOYZN GIRLS,' it said. 'THIS IS A BIG DAY FOR ALL OF US. IT'S A GIG. IT'S A NEW LOOK. IT'S AN ALBUM-RECORDING SESSION. LAZEN GEM'MEN BOYZN

GIRLS, IT IS . . . DEATH ERIC LIVE AT CASTLE BONES!'

Rustic heyho music. Green smoke drifted over the backstage area. There would be masses of it billowing on to the stage.

'Vot is this stupidness?' said Vlad, blowing a septic cloud of smoke. 'Ah. Erik. I vill be singink lead vocals for you today.'

'Oh. Yeah,' said Eric, still arranging bat claws and nodding, possibly because he was not listening, but more probably because the idea of Vlad singing lead vocals was too silly to show up on his radar.

'Sing?' said Enid, looking heartbroken. 'You?'

Vlad batted his ghastly eyelashes at her. 'A man in loff can do anythink,' he said.

'Oo, *Vlad*!' said Enid, turning stoplight red and buckling at the knees.

Onstage, Kenyatta and Fingers had been greeted with mighty roars of applause, and were now settled into a heavy freight-train groove.

'So I vill sing lead vocals,' said Vlad. 'Then Death Eric vill support Honganian Folk Orchestra in New Look shattering climax. OK?'

'Hee-hee,' said Eric, who had now decided it was

a joke and had doubled up with laughter. 'Oo you are a one, Vlad.'

'He's serious,' hissed Buddy.

'Course he isn't!' said Eric. 'He can't be!' With a final snort of laughter, he ran on to the stage. The crowd roared. Rabid Dingo began to howl the opening riff of 'Chainsaw'.

'All *right*,' said Buddy and Lou. Stuffing earplugs into their ears, they went to watch from the wings.

'Chainsaw' was going beautifully. The band was tight, tight, *tight*. Night was falling. The lake was a blank sheet in the foreground, scattered with the lanterns of canoeists. Behind it the audience spread up the slopes from the water's edge, roaring a long, enthusiastic roar.

'Chainsaw' came to an end with Kenyatta sawing Fingers' bass in half. The crowd went mad, obviously. Fingers strapped on a new guitar and the band started in on 'Doom Lagoon' in a howl of feedback and a thunder of drums. At this exact moment, Buddy's telephone started to vibrate. The screen said GOTHALINDA.

He beckoned Lou. They ducked into the sound-proof room the recording engineers had built.

'Yeah?' said Buddy.

'Dollink!' cried a familiar voice. 'Vot is happenink?'

'It's a festival,' said Buddy. 'Where are you?'

'I've got no idea!' cried Gothalinda. 'All these *people*!'

'Are you in Smoke City?'

'No, no. Drat.' The line went dead.

'Buddy,' said Lou. 'Look.'

Death Eric were thundering along to the delight of all. But in the dark place behind the amplifiers, there was movement. Little people in fur hats were milling about. A long thing caught the light: the neck of an ood.

'It's the Honganians!' said Buddy. 'Come on!'

Stuffing the phone into his pocket, he rushed into the backstage area.

The Honganians were dancing a tragically sad ring-a-ring o'roses. Every now and then, one of them shot several metres in the air with his arms folded.

'Get Enid!' shouted Lou.

Buddy ran for Enid. He saw her print shoulders towering above the crowd backstage.

'Enid!' he yelled. 'It's Vlad! He's going to sing! Stop him!'

'What?' said Enid, dazed.

The telephone in Buddy's pocket rang again. 'Yeah?' he said.

'Dollink,' said Gothalinda.

'Where *are* you?' said Buddy. 'Can you get to Castle Bones?'

'But I am *here*!' said the voice.

'Wha.'

'At the gate. But there are many peoples, like I said, and big fat mens with SECURITATE –'

'– security –'

'– like I said, written on their T-shirts, and they vill not let me in, and they are frightening the horses, so I think I vill go home.'

'DON'T GO!' shouted Buddy. 'STAY! WE'LL SEND SOMEONE! DON'T GO!'

'Go where?' said Enid, pitching up alongside him.

'Enid,' said Buddy. 'Thank goodness. There's a black carriage with four black horses up at the main gate. Send someone to bring it down, all right? Oh, and Vlad and the Honganians are going to sing with the band.'

'The band?'

'Death Eric.'

'Fan*tastic*!' said Enid, her eyes lighting up with one million candlepower of pure love.

'Rrr,' said Buddy. 'Not *so*!'

*

The band had played 'Doom Lagoon' (new). They had played 'Dead Cat Bounce' (new). They were finishing off 'Bat Soup'(new). Eric was two metres in the air, prior to coming down on the pedal with the bang that would kick the band into the outro, when he noticed a small person in baggy trousers and a fur hat skipping between him and the stage. Eric lived outside most laws, but gravity was not one of them.

He came down like an avalanche with a black guitar and purple hair. 'Oof!' said the Honganian, flattened. Eric rolled backwards, escaping, slithering across the stage, his guitar making a huge jangling noise. He tried to work out what if anything had gone wrong, or whether it was part of the stage act that someone had told him about and he had already forgotten. But it was not easy to work things out.

This was because the whole stage now seemed to be covered in Honganians. There was a worrying number of ood and skveezebox players, and someone setting up a pie stove in the corner. Eric's mind filled with the smell of sour milk. Yuk, he thought. And with that yuk came a feeling of greater yuk, for Honganian musicians and the horrible noises they made. Eric did not want them on his nice live album. He groped for his guitar and slung it round himself. A roadie came to plug it in. The crowd was going mental. They thought it was all part of the act. Well, for all Eric knew it was.

Then he saw It. It was wearing a cloak as usual. It also had on high black boots and a big feeble type hat with silver stuff round it. It was like . . . *stalking* . . . up to the *mike stand*. To *Eric*'s mike stand.

Not It. Er Vlad.

'Oi!' shouted Eric.

Er Vlad did not look at him.

'Oi!' shouted Eric again, looking into the wings. And, sure enough, there was Enid, large as life if not somewhat larger, staring at er Vlad as if er Vlad was a pie. With beans. That she planned to eat. Like slowly. After a long walk in a foodless desert . . .

Eric's head filled up with pictures of camels and palm trees, and he heard his guitar play the theme from *Lawrence of Arabia*.

Someone was pulling at his singlet. He looked down. He saw his son er Lou and his daughter er Buddy. Or the other way round. They were pointing. At big bits of paper they had in. Their hands. With. Writing on. PLAY BAD SKOOOL, said Buddy's bit of paper.

Eric frowned. He loved his children and wanted to do his best four. Not four. For. Them. But he did not think it was a father's job to be told. So he looked at the set list nailed to the stage by the pedal. BA, he read. DSKOOOL. It sounded enough like Buddy's idea to be OK.

'OK,' he said. Fingers was looking at him. Kenyatta was looking at him.

Someone was waving a bit of paper under his nose. He looked down. It was his daughter er Lou er Buddy er Lou. The bit of paper said PLAY A RONG KORD.

'No,' said Eric.

He grasped his pick, positioned his fingers, put a foot forward and started the long whining note at the beginning of 'Bad Skoool'. The roar of the crowd stilled. The head banging on all sides was like the tossing of a mighty sea –

Lou turned over her bit of paper. GO ON, it said.

'No,' said Eric, and turned away, heading for the mike stand.

But the mike stand was already occupied by the

tall, cloaked figure of Vlad. Vlad had one hand on the mike, and the other in the air. He was making oily gestures with the one in the air. His mouth was open. Any second now he was going to introduce himself as Eric's New Look. And then he was going to start singing.

Nooooo, howled Eric soundlessly in the din. And because his voice and his guitar were exactly the same thing, his fingers slithered all the way from the top of the fretboard to the bottom, producing a noise somewhere between Jimi Hendrix and an earthquake.

It was a fantastic sound, never made before or since. But as far as 'Bad Skoool' was concerned it was definitely a wrong chord. Vlad looked round nervously. Eric said, 'Off,' and waved him away with his guitar neck, still playing the 'Bad Skoool' riff. Vlad curled a thin lip, flicked his hair away from his eyes and drew breath to sing.

Something happened.

Back in the wings, Buddy and Lou found they were wrinkling their noses at a truly awful swamp-and-sewage smell. Then a streak of bright-pink light whizzed on to the stage and coiled four times round Eric's microphone stand. The tip of the light streak turned into an enormous boxing glove, which drew back and waited, shuddering a bit, opposite Vlad's handsome features.

The fist darted forward and smacked Vlad straight in the chops.

'BOOF!' cried a mighty voice.

Vlad cartwheeled away into the darkness. The pink thing round the mike stand shimmered a bit, then condensed. And there stood a man with red hair, an electric-green suit and lizardskin cowboy boots with the lizards' heads still on the toes and barking like dogs. A man two metres tall. A man with a thin face and bony hands, all right: but a man, not a skeleton. A man who looked pretty weird, particularly if you looked at his eyes, which were blood-red and shaved the air like searchlights. A man who picked up the mike stand in both hands, rose from the ground and glided slowly out over the black waters of the lake, in which he left no reflection.

A man who started singing 'Bad Skoool' as if he had written it.

Which of course he had.

It was the New Material. And the New Look. And the old Death Eric on tiptop form.

The crowd went mad.

*

'Wow,' said Buddy.

'Cool,' said Lou.

It was some show.

That went for what was happening onstage, too.

But what the Thrashmettle children were watching was happening at the edge of the lake.

Vlad was swimming towards the land. Enid was striding round the water's edge to give succour to her beloved. And down through the crowd, drawn by a team of night-black horses, there ploughed a black carriage with a small but hairy driver.

Vlad got to the land and stood looking like a drowned bat. He beckoned the carriage, which clattered along the rim, the coachman lashing the horses, scattering metal fans left and right. The coach stopped. A dark woman in a tight blood-red gown stepped out and threw a look of deep scorn at Vlad. But Vlad did not see it, as he had immediately clasped her in his arms.

It was at this point that Enid arrived on the scene, wearing her dumb Love Hypnotized smile.

For a moment she watched the couple. Then she tapped Vlad on the shoulder. Then Vlad turned round and said something that even at a range of fifty metres the children could tell was not even slightly polite. Then Enid's face stopped looking Love Hypnotized and started looking extremely tough. Then Enid tore Vlad free of Gothalinda, who thanked her very much. Then Enid shifted her grip to Vlad's ankle, swung him three times round her head, and slung him as far as she could into the lake.

Which, dear reader, was a good long way.

The Ghost made huge wheel-winding movements with his right hand. Death Eric howled into the solo. Buddy swiped a walkie-talkie off a stage hand, selected Enid's channel and pressed the TALK button.

'Wha,' said Enid's voice, dazed and crackly.

'Bring Gothalinda back here,' said Buddy. 'Then make it happen.'

'Make wha happen.'

'What we said.'

'Oh,' said Enid. 'That twotiming goodfornuthin' homewrecking bloodsucker.'

'Exactly.'

'Children,' said Enid. 'Please accept my apologies. I have been blind.'

'Love is a weird thing, very close to illness of the mind,' said Buddy.

'*Buddy!*' said Lou, shocked. 'Enid, we accept your apologies. Welcome home!'

'Lou!' cried Enid.

'Enid!' cried Lou.

'Enid!' cried Buddy.

'Buddy!' cried Enid.

'Enough already!' cried Gothalinda. 'Some peoples got vork to do, innit?'

'Oops,' said Enid. 'Gotta go.' She shot off in a direction.

Up on the stage, the band played on. Over the lake, the Ghost did its mighty dance, singing from time to time in harmony with itself. It was raining now, but the crowd was so hot that the rain turned to steam and drifted away, so Castle Bones was dry, though down the road in Smoke City people were complaining about the fog.

In the backstage area, mighty engines rumbled.

'Wait for the last chorus,' said Enid into her walkie-talkie. 'Here it comes. Three. Two. One. *Yep.*'

As she said 'Yep', men took the thermal covers off six huge tipper lorries. The lorries reversed up to the lake's rim. As Eric played a blinding solo and the Ghost did the Octopus Dance, the lorries tipped their loads of dry ice into deep water.

The lake began to boil.

'Right,' said Lou, looking at the bit of paper in her hand. 'Raven next.'

'Check,' said Buddy, unlatching the door of the large cage. 'Remember, raven, fly over the lake. After that your time's your own.'

'Chark,' said the Raven, with a dry rattle of feathers. It waddled to the edge of the cage, hopped up on to the door sill, and launched itself into the night.

'OK,' said Lou. 'We're on.'

'Will they let us?' said Buddy.

Scheming behind the scenes was one thing. Being eleven years old and talking to a quarter of a million people was another.

'Enid?' said Lou. 'Will they let us?'

'I'd like to see them try to stop you,' said Enid.

On to the stage they marched.

The raven was putting in a bit of wheeling time. It was an interesting scene. Noisy, granted, but OK if you liked the music. Ravens are not into music, much. But they like stuff that glitters, and they are curious birds.

This is what the raven saw and heard (though obviously it understood very little).

Two children walked on to the stage, followed by an enormous woman in a print dress. The lights were flashing red and green. Searchlights played over the crowd, flicking across the boiling water of the lake. The Ghost drifted back to the stage. It seemed to be watching the children. Watching hopefully. The music was roaring.

'Bring it down,' said a child's voice.

The music came down.

'Ghost,' said the child's voice (Lou's voice, though obviously the raven did not know this) through a microphone, 'in fulfilment of the ancient rhyme, you will henceforth be known as Death Aluminium Dave Krang. This I tell you because our dad has given you the Death from Death Eric, who will from now on be known as Eric. Dad?'

'Cool,' said Eric.

Twing, went the air by the raven's ear, as if tight stitches had somehow been cut.

'The lake,' said Lou, 'is boiling. In er fulfilment of the ancient rhyme.'

Twing, went the air by the raven's ear, as if more tight stitches had somehow been cut.

'And now,' said Lou, 'all that remains is this: do we love Death Aluminium Dave Krang? Tell him we love him!'

'We love you!' roared the crowd. Well, some of the crowd. But not all the crowd, because metal fans are purists, which means that if they have paid to hear Death Eric they feel they have been robbed if they find themselves hearing a band that seems to be called Eric with some ghost on lead vocals.

'Louder!' shouted Lou.

'WE LOVE YOU!' roared 249,997 of the crowd.

'LOUDER.'

'*WE LOVE YOU!*' roared 249,998 of the crowd.

'WHAT?'

'WE LOVE YOU!'

'*WHAT?*'

'WE LOVE YOU!' roared 249,999 of the crowd.

But this time, the raven said it too.

And in the raven's ear the *twing* of cut stitches turned into a huge, celestial chord of splendid music.

And down on the stage, the Ghost looked at Lou and smiled a really lovely smile. Then it turned long and thin and headed straight up into the sky. In which the rain clouds had parted like two enormous doors, giving way to a deep dome of black velvet in which stars twinkled warm and yellow.

'Job done,' said the raven.

It spread the finger-feathers on its wings and cruised down to sit in the top of a yew tree. Eric was its favourite band. And unless it was badly mistaken, that was the introduction to 'Pig Train'.

OUTRO

It was a week later. Everyone was having lunch on the terrace at Castle Bones. Not the same everyone as a week ago, of course. There were Lou and Buddy, obviously. And Eric, and Fingers, and Kenyatta. And Enid, and various members of the entourage, and Gothalinda lying in a heavily carved chair sipping tomato juice through a straw.

Since the Ghost had gone, it seemed that (as promised) the Castle Bones Curse had gone too.

The weather had got better. Once the drizzle had stopped, the slimy paving stones of the terrace had turned out to be a nice place with stone railings round it, and a stone table, and a fine sweep of ground heading down to a couple of ornamental temples. Wild flowers were flowering all over the place. A rainbow arched over the yew woods, and a flock of brilliant parrots passed overhead, arguing about their favourite kinds of nut.

'Quite a difference,' said Gothalinda, wrinkling her nose. 'Looking like scene off cereal packet or shampoo commercial.'

'You don't like it?' said Lou.

'I have very nice ruined palace in Eastern Approaches now,' said Gothalinda. 'I shall be returning there today.'

'Enid'll give you a lift to the airport,' said Buddy.

'Airport, shmairport. Boris has the horses ready.'

'It'll take you a year.'

'What is vun year in seven hundred and twenty-two? Style,' said Gothalinda, 'is everything.' She rose. 'Bye bye, everyvun.'

Everyone kissed her goodbye. Buddy tried to do the minimum, because though beautiful she was very powdery and her perfume made his eyes water.

Lou hugged her in an arm's length sort of way. Revamp or no revamp, she did not want those sharp teeth anywhere near her neck.

'Well,' said Fingers ten minutes later, as Gothalinda's horses dragged her up the drive. 'Let's see the album cover, then.'

Out it came. 𝕰𝖗𝖎𝖈, said the Gothic lettering. 𝖀𝖓𝖉𝖊𝖆𝖉 𝖆𝖙 𝕮𝖆𝖘𝖙𝖑𝖊 𝕭𝖔𝖓𝖊𝖘. The rest of it was ghosts, castles and lakes, obviously. 𝖋𝖊𝖆𝖙𝖚𝖗𝖎𝖓𝖌 𝖙𝖍𝖊 𝖌𝖍𝖔𝖘𝖙 𝖔𝖋 𝕯𝖊𝖆𝖙𝖍 𝕬𝖑𝖚𝖒𝖎𝖓𝖎𝖚𝖒 𝕯𝖆𝖛𝖊 𝕶𝖗𝖆𝖓𝖌, said more lettering.

'Lovely,' said everyone, meaning it.

'And the record company's very pleased,' said Enid, looking shiftily away, as she tended to since the flight of Vlad. 'It's been a total relaunch. They want to talk to the management about another five years' contract, with loadsa wonga.'

'Yeah,' said Eric. 'Great.'

'But you haven't got a management,' said Enid.

'What about Valve the Fags, whatever, cloak teeth wally?' said Eric.

'Vlad has gone back to his castle in Hongania,' said Enid, blushing furiously. 'The creep. With all his pies and his ood players and that.'

'Bad news geezer,' said Buddy.

'Oh,' said Eric. Pause. 'Well, Enid.'

'Enid wha.'

'That's your name, right?'

'Yes,' said Enid patiently.

'Well, the geezer before was nicking money type rubbish. And the geezer after the geezer before was talk the talk but not walk the walk type rubbish. And the geezer after the geezer before who was after the geezer before him was, like, I wanna suck your blood or maybe not and then sing flat type rubbish. So they were all rubbish. And you're not.'

'What?' said Enid, very pale.

'He wants you to be it,' said Buddy.

'The Management,' said Lou.

'Yeah,' said Eric.

'Great,' said Fingers.

'Fine,' said Kenyatta.

'But I'm a girl,' said Enid, looking pink, beautiful, gigantic and extremely proud.

'Gimme a *break*,' said Lou.

'All right,' said Enid, brushing away a tear of joy. 'I'll do it, then.'

'It'll be a disaster,' said Sid the Soothsayer.

Buddy looked at Lou. Lou looked at Buddy. 'Happy ever after, then,' they said.

Puffin by Post

The Haunting of Death Eric

If you have enjoyed this book and want to read more,
then check out these other great Puffin titles.
You can order any of the following books direct with Puffin by Post: